THE VENGEANCE OF VICKERY

THE VENGEANCE OF VICKERY

When, after a lengthy absence, Lee Vickery returns to his parents' Box V Ranch in the Texas Panhandle, he finds that they have both died, and that the ranch is in the hands of wealthy, unscrupulous rancher Mort Cooney, who owns the adjacent Circle D spread. He soon begins to suspect that the death of his mother and the loss of the ranch are the result of criminal activities on the part of Cooney and his hired gunslingers. Can Vickery prove this and deliver the guilty parties to the law, even with the help of an old friend?

The Vengeance Of Vickery

by

Alan Irwin

Dales Large Print Books
Long Preston, North Yorkshire,
BD23 4ND, England.

British Library Cataloguing in Publication Data.

Irwin, Alan
  The vengeance of Vickery.

  A catalogue record of this book is
  available from the British Library

  ISBN 1-84262-385-0 pbk

First published in Great Britain 2004 by Robert Hale Limited

Cover illustration © Longaron by arrangement with
Norma Editorial S.A.

Published in Large Print 2005 by arrangement with
Robert Hale Limited

Dales Large Print is an imprint of Library Magna Books Ltd.

Printed and bound in Great Britain by
T.J. (International) Ltd., Cornwall, PL28 8RW

ONE

Lee Vickery saw the ranch house and out-buildings as he topped the rise. He paused, and looked down into the valley below. The buildings stood about a mile distant, close to the stream which snaked along between the slopes leading to the high ground on either side. The valley, as far as the eye could see, was well stocked with grazing cows.

Lee was sure, from the description given to him in a letter from his mother, that he was looking at the Box V ranch, established two years earlier by his parents Dan and Martha Vickery in the Texas Panhandle, north of Amarillo and not far from the border with Indian Territory.

Martha had described the bend in the stream which almost half-circled the build-ings, and the small grove of trees standing

7

not far from the house.

He rode down into the valley, and ten minutes later passed under the timber arch roughly branded with the inscription BOX V RANCH. He rode towards the buildings. As he drew closer he spotted various signs of neglect about the place, and there was no one visible around the buildings. Nor could he see any horses.

He dismounted outside the house and knocked several times on the door. There was no reply. He opened the door and walked inside, to find that although all the rooms were furnished, it was apparent that nobody had lived there for some time.

He looked in the desk and the cupboards in the living-room. Items were still stowed away inside. In the bedroom there were clothes in the wardrobe, and in a big chest standing on the floor there were a couple of blankets.

He went outside to look at the barn and the other outbuildings; it was clear that they had not been in use for some time.

He returned to his horse, and stood by it

for a short while, puzzled by the fact that although the ranch buildings appeared to have been abandoned, there were still cattle on the nearby range. Suddenly, he felt a strong sense of foreboding. He mounted his horse and headed for the town of Bledsoe which, according to his mother's letter, was five miles further down the valley.

It was late afternoon by the time he reached Bledsoe. He could see that it had the usual amenities of a medium-sized frontier town. Riding along the main street, on the look-out for the general store, he passed the hotel, blacksmith shop, saloon and restaurant. He noticed that on the large sign attached to the front of each of these establishments, the name of the proprietor was shown as MORT COONEY.

Obviously, thought Lee, this man Cooney must be an important and influential member of the community.

As he passed the restaurant, he noticed the general store ahead, on his right, and the bank and livery stable further along, on his left. For a change, the sign on the front of the store showed the name of the proprietor to be SETH WEBSTER.

Lee rode up to the store, dismounted, and tied his horse to the hitching rail. He stood for a moment on the boardwalk, recalling what his mother had written in her letter about the storekeeper and his wife Abigail. They had, she wrote, become very good friends, and the four of them met regularly.

He opened the door of the store and stepped inside. A middle-aged man was standing behind the counter, and a woman of similar age was occupied at the back of the store stacking goods on the shelves.

Webster, a pleasant-faced man of medium height, looked up as Lee approached the counter. He had the odd feeling that he had encountered this stranger before, but he couldn't think where or when. He studied Lee closely.

The man he saw before him was in his early thirties, tall, fair-haired, clean-shaven and well-built. He had a strong face, square-chinned, with a small scar on his cheek.

'Howdy,' said Lee. 'Maybe you can help me. I was riding through the valley from the west when I passed the ranch buildings on the Box V. They all looked like they'd been abandoned. There was nobody around. D'you know what happened to the folks who were running the spread?'

Abigail Webster, hearing the question, stopped what she was doing, and walked up to stand by Lee at the counter as her husband replied.

'The Box V,' he said, 'until four months ago, was run by Dan and Martha Vickery, both good friends of ours. Then Dan took ill with cholera, and in a week he was dead.

'Martha took it real bad, but she kept the place running, with the help of the three ranch hands that Dan took on when he started ranching here five years back. Then, about a month after Dan died, we lost Martha as well.'

He paused, sensing the deep shock felt by the stranger at his words.

'She took sick?' asked Lee.

'No,' Webster replied. 'We couldn't believe what happened. For a while, it looked like she was getting over the shock of losing Dan. Then, one day, a ranch hand found her in the house with a bullet wound in the side of her head, and Dan's six-gun lying on the floor close to the body. It looked like she'd killed herself.'

'Never!' said Lee. 'My mother was one of the strongest women I know.'

The storekeeper and his wife stared at him.

'Your mother!' said Abigail Webster. 'Then you're Lee?'

Lee nodded.

'We're very sorry,' she said, 'that you've turned up to find that both your parents have died. It's been a big shock to us as well. Martha told us all about you hankering to see more of the country before you settled down to help them on the ranch. She reckoned it wouldn't be long before you came home.

'When Dan died, she wanted to let you know, but she didn't know where you were.'

'That's right,' said Lee. 'She knew I was figuring on drifting around for a while before I finally headed for home. I can't believe that she killed herself. She just wasn't like that.'

'That's just how we felt,' said Abigail Webster, 'but there didn't seem to be any other explanation.'

'Was there a suicide note?' asked Lee.

'No,' replied the storekeeper, 'and the hands said she was acting normal when they rode out on to the range early that morning.'

'Where are they buried?' asked Lee.

'We took care of things,' said Webster. 'They're lying together on the side of a knoll not far from the ranch house. They used to sit there sometimes. We figured they'd like to be there.

'We marked each of the graves with a stout timber cross, sunk well down, with the name on it. And there's a strong fence around the graves, with a gate in it.'

'I'm real obliged to you for that,' said Lee, still shaken by the news. 'I'll ride back there and take a look. I guess I'd better start thinking about what I'm going to do with the ranch.

'I'm not sure I want to run it for myself. I served as a deputy sheriff in Kansas for nigh on a year, and the job seemed to suit me. Maybe I'll sell up here and take up a lawman's job again.'

Webster glanced at his wife, then spoke to Lee.

'You ain't heard all the bad news yet,' he said. 'The Box V's been taken over by a man called Mort Cooney.'

Shocked, Lee stared at the storekeeper.

'How could that happen?' he asked. 'I remember seeing that name on buildings along the street. Are you talking about the man who seems to own most of the businesses in town?'

'The same,' said Webster. 'I figure you know that your father liked to sit in a game of poker now and then. And I know he was a good player. Every now and then he sat in a game at Cooney's saloon.

'About a month after your mother died,

Cooney produced an IOU that he said was signed by your father during a poker game, and which transferred the Box V land, buildings and contents, and cattle, to Cooney. The poker game took place the evening before your father was took ill with the cholera.

'Cooney's story was that he didn't produce the IOU while your mother was still alive, because he didn't want to cause her more worry at the time. But anybody who knows Cooney will tell you that he's never shown an ounce of sympathy for anybody but himself.'

'My father would never have signed the ranch away like that,' said Lee. 'Sure, he liked a game of poker, but he was a cautious player. He would never have played for a stake as high as that. That IOU must have been forged.'

'That's what Abigail and me, and a lot of other folks in town thought,' said Webster, 'but it turned out that Maxwell, who manages the bank here, was sitting in the poker game. The other players were your father,

Cooney and a man called Martin who's employed by Cooney as his ramrod out at the ranch.

'Maxwell's pretty well respected in town, and he said he saw your father write out the IOU and sign it. So Cooney took the Box V over. He already owned the big Circle D ranch further down the valley. He bought that from the owner's widow when the owner died three years ago.

'Dan told us a while before he died, that Cooney had made him an offer for the Box V. Your father told him that the last thing he had in mind was selling the ranch, because he and Abigail were well-suited with the place, and were looking forward to you coming along and helping them run it.'

'This man Cooney,' asked Lee, 'does anybody know anything about his past?'

'Not a thing,' Webster replied. 'He turned up here out of the blue, with what appeared like an endless supply of money. It weren't long after he got here that he bought the Circle D. The ranch house is a few miles east of here. Then he built the hotel and the restaurant next door, and by keeping his prices low for the time being, he soon put Emma Duncan, a widow who ran a boarding-house in town, out of business.

'Not long after that, he built the saloon and opened it, then he brought a man in to run a proper blacksmith shop for him. It seems like he's figuring on taking over the whole town.'

'You reckon he might be aiming to take over some of the other businesses in town as well?' asked Lee.

'I think it's possible,' Webster replied. 'Abigail and me, we're scared that he'll decide to build himself a store, and start undercutting our prices, which would put us out of business.'

'Those three ranch hands who used to work on the Box V,' asked Lee, 'are any of them still around?'

'Only Todd Weaver,' Webster replied. 'The other two headed for south Texas to look for work on one of the big ranches down there.

Todd's been helping me out part-time in the store, but I've got a feeling he'll be heading south himself before long. He was the one who found your mother dead.

'If you'd like a word with him, I'm expecting him to turn up any time now.'

'Yes, I'd like to speak with him,' said Lee.

Weaver arrived a few minutes later, and Webster introduced him to Lee, explaining that before his arrival, Lee was not aware of the deaths of his parents.

'I guess it's been a big shock to you,' said Weaver, 'and me and the other hands took it pretty bad. We all liked working on the Box V.'

'I'd like a few words with you about what happened,' said Lee.

'Sure,' said Weaver. The two men walked out of the store on to the boardwalk as a customer entered.

'Mr Webster tells me you found my mother after she'd been shot,' said Lee.

'That's right,' said Weaver, 'and it sure shook me up for a while.'

'D'you think she shot herself?' asked Lee.

18

'I just couldn't believe it,' Weaver replied. 'It had seemed to all of us that she was getting over the shock of losing your father, and she'd started talking about looking forward to you turning up here to help her out.

'When the three of us left her that morning to ride out on to the range, we talked about how it looked like she was getting back to normal at last.'

'The six-gun lying on the floor beside her was my father's?' asked Lee.

'It was his all right,' replied Weaver. 'There was a mark on the handle that I'd seen before. But there was one thing puzzled me. The day before your father was took ill, he told me he was plumb out of ammunition for the Colt. He said he'd used up his last round, and he was aiming to get some more the next time he was in town. But he never got to town again.

'When I looked at the six-gun I found lying beside your mother, I saw that only one chamber had been loaded and fired, and I wondered how she'd come by that one cartridge. I couldn't find any more in the house.'

Lee thanked Weaver, and a little later, he spoke with the Websters in their living-quarters, while Weaver minded the store.

'Like I told you before,' he said, 'there are two things I'll never believe. The first is that my father would gamble his ranch away. The second is that my mother would take her own life. I'm staying on here till I find out exactly what did happen. I'll take a room at the hotel.'

'You'll do no such thing,' said Abigail Webster. 'We've got a spare room, and you're welcome to it for as long as you like. Your mother was my best friend around here.'

'I'm obliged to you,' said Lee.

A little later, he asked the storekeeper whether his mother had, during the last few weeks of her life, bought any ammunition from the store.

'No, she didn't,' Webster replied, 'and I don't remember the last time your father did.'

TWO

The following morning Lee rose early and rode out to the place where his father and mother had been buried. For a long while he stood by the graves, then he rode back to town. During his stay on the knoll, there had been no signs of life around the ranch buildings.

He tied his horse to the hitching rail outside the bank, and walked inside. An elderly teller was sitting behind the counter, waiting for the next customer to appear. Lee walked up to him.

'I'd like to see Mr Maxwell,' he said.

'I'll see if he's free,' said the teller. 'What name should I say?'

'Lee Vickery,' Lee replied, 'son of Dan Vickery of the Box V.'

The teller left, and returned after a few

minutes. He led Lee to a small room at the rear of the building and ushered him inside, then returned to the counter.

Maxwell was seated behind a desk. He rose to his feet as Lee entered. He was a slim, well-dressed man of medium height, in his early sixties. His beard and moustache were neatly trimmed. He observed Lee keenly, before speaking.

'Please accept my commiserations on the deaths of your parents, Mr Vickery,' he said. 'They will be sorely missed. Your father was a valued customer of this bank. Is there any way I can help you?'

'That business of the IOU that my father handed to Mr Cooney,' said Lee. 'I'm finding it mighty hard to believe that he would take the risk of losing the ranch in a card game. But I understand that you saw him write the IOU and hand it over.'

'That's right,' said the banker. 'I read what was on the IOU, and I must say I was very surprised. I'd played in poker games with your father before, and I never saw him play such a reckless game as he did that evening.'

'When my mother died,' asked Lee, 'did she leave any money deposited in the bank?'

'I'm afraid not,' said Maxwell. 'There was a small balance when your father died, but she withdrew it all soon after.'

The banker stood up. 'Let me know if I can help you in any way,' he said.

Outside the bank, Lee stood on the board-walk for a moment or two, thinking. The banker had appeared quite confident about the authenticity of the IOU, but Lee thought that he had detected a note of unease on Maxwell's part during their conversation.

He walked back to the store for a midday meal with the Websters. After the meal, the storekeeper and his wife went into the store, leaving Lee alone in the living-room. A few minutes later, Webster reappeared with a stranger, a short, smartly dressed, middle-aged man, stocky and bearded. Hard eyes, set in a bleak, ruthless face, took stock of Lee.

'This is Mr Cooney, Lee,' said Webster.

'He'd like a few words with you.'

He went back into the store, leaving the two men alone. With an effort, Cooney creased his face into the faint semblance of a smile as he shook hands with Lee.

'I'm here,' he said, 'to say how sorry I am about the deaths of your parents. And on top of that, you've had the shock of finding out that there's no ranch for you to take over.

'We couldn't figure out what got into your father, but in this town, a gambling debt has got to be repaid.'

'Nobody could quarrel with that,' said Lee. 'If there *was* a gambling debt, it needed to be repaid. It's just that I knew my father well enough to find it mighty hard to believe that he'd risk losing his ranch over a game of cards.'

The semblance of a smile disappeared from Cooney's face. He took a piece of paper from his pocket and handed it to Lee.

'I don't like what you're saying, Vickery,' he said. 'You must know that Maxwell, the banker, was a witness when the IOU was handed over. Take a good look at it. Then your best plan would be to leave the valley pronto. There's nothing here for you now, and if you go on shooting off your mouth like you just did, you'll be in deep trouble.'

Lee closely examined the IOU. The writing on it, and the signature, were similar to that of his father. He handed it back to Cooney.

'I aim to hang around for a while,' he said. 'There's a lot of questions still to be answered.'

Cooney's face darkened with anger. 'You've been warned,' he said, harshly. 'Don't interfere in my affairs.'

He turned abruptly, stomped into the store, and out of the building.

Lee followed him into the store, and told the Websters about his conversation with Cooney.

'Having met the man,' he went on, 'I have the feeling that he's just a natural-born, greedy liar, who got his hands on the Box V by trickery. Maybe it's going to be hard to prove that. But that's what I aim to try and do.'

'You're going to have to watch out for yourself,' warned Webster. 'I think that Cooney's a dangerous man. And he's got some hands out at the ranch who look more like gunslingers than cowhands.'

'The trouble is,' said Lee, 'that I don't have much idea of where to start looking for evidence against Cooney. You told me that the fourth player in the poker game was Cooney's ramrod, so it ain't likely he'll contradict his boss. Maybe somebody else in the saloon at the time saw what happened.'

'I already checked up on that,' said the storekeeper. 'A couple of friends of mine were in the saloon at the time, sitting at another table, but they were too far away to notice an IOU going into the pot.

'But they said that when your father quit the game to go back to the ranch, he smiled and waved to them just like he did any other time. He didn't act like a man who'd just gambled his ranch away.'

When Cooney returned to the room, built on to the back of the saloon, which he used as an office and a bedroom when he was in town, he sat down at his desk, still seething from his encounter with Lee. He decided that if Dan Vickery's son made a nuisance of himself, he would have to get rid of him.

In the saloon itself, which was empty of customers at the time, Cooney's two saloon girls, Alice and Kate, were seated at a table. The girls had been enticed by Cooney, during a visit he had made to Amarillo three months previously, to leave a big saloon there, on the promise of higher earnings at his own saloon in Bledsoe.

But on arrival in Bledsoe, they were sadly disillusioned. Cooney had insisted on taking all their earnings and handing back only a small proportion, so that they were living a hand-to-mouth existence, with no hope of accumulating any savings.

Both girls badly wanted to quit, and return to Amarillo, but Cooney had threatened violence if they tried to leave, and they knew that they were being closely watched. Also, they did not have sufficient money to cover the cost of the journey.

'I'm getting desperate,' said Kate. 'I've got to get away from here.'

'You're no keener to get away than I am,' said Alice, 'but what can we do about it? You got any ideas?'

'I've been thinking about what we might do,' Kate replied. 'You know that Vickery's son turned up in town?'

'Yes,' Alice replied. 'I heard the barkeep talking about it. Seems like he's staying at the store.'

'That's right,' said Kate. 'Now there's something I ain't told you about. You remember that on the day Mrs Vickery died, a stranger came into the saloon in the evening, asking for Cooney. He was a tall, slim man, with cold eyes, and the look of a gunfighter about him. He had a scar just above his right eye. I heard Cooney call him Brady.'

'I remember him,' said Alice. 'I figured

that Cooney had hired him for some job he wanted doing.'

'You figured right,' said Kate. 'I saw Cooney take him up to the room next to mine, and I was curious about what sort of business they might be in together. So I went upstairs and climbed out of my room window on to the veranda. I listened at the next window.

'It was open a little, and I could hear them talking. I heard Cooney ask Brady how he'd killed the Vickery woman. Brady said he'd shot her in the side of the head, using a gun he'd found in the house. He'd left the gun on the floor, against her hand, to make it look like suicide.

'Cooney told Brady that he'd hand him the payment for the job before he left the next morning. Then he told Brady how, with the banker's help in forging an IOU, he had a story ready about winning the Box V from Dan Vickery in a poker-game. So, with Martha Vickery dead, there was nothing now to stop him from taking the Box V over.

'Just then, one of them closed the window, and I couldn't hear any more. So I went back into my own room.'

'You've got me more scared now than I was before,' said Alice. 'We've just *got* to get away from here.'

'I've just had an idea,' said Kate. 'If I can let Vickery know what I heard when I was listening to Cooney and Brady, maybe he'll help us to get away from here.

'Things are pretty quiet in here this evening, and I reckon we'll be able to go to our rooms around eleven thirty. Then we can go to the store to see Vickery.'

'But how're we going to get out without anybody knowing?' asked Alice.

'There's a ladder lying on the veranda outside my room,' Kate replied. 'It's being used by the man who's painting the outside of the saloon. We can use it to climb down to that alley running along the side of the saloon. We'll have to travel light, and that means leaving most of our clothes behind. Are you game, Alice?'

'Anything's better than staying here,' Alice replied. 'I'm game. When do we leave?'

'Just after midnight would be a good time,' said Kate. 'There ain't likely to be anybody on the street at that time.'

The girls went to their rooms at half past eleven and hurriedly changed their clothes. They each stuffed into a carpetbag the items they wanted to take with them. Then they climbed out of the window on to the veranda.

They picked up the ladder, and placed it so that its foot was standing in the alley below. Kate stood on a chair, stepped over the veranda rail on to the ladder, and climbed down to the ground. Alice dropped the two carpetbags down to Kate, then followed her.

After laying the ladder on the ground the two girls walked along the alley and scanned the street in both directions. It was deserted. They hurried across the street towards the general store, which was in darkness, and went to the door of the living-quarters at the rear of the building.

Kate had to knock repeatedly before a

light showed from inside. This was followed by the opening of the door. Webster stood in the doorway, holding a lamp. His jaw dropped as he recognized Kate and Alice.

'Mr Webster,' said Kate, urgently. 'We want to see Mr Vickery. There's some things we can tell him about how his mother died, and about that poker-game that his father sat in with Cooney. Can we come in, please?'

Webster stepped back inside, and beckoned them in. He took them to the living-room, where they sat down while Webster went for Lee. He returned with Lee shortly after and introduced him to the two women.

Lee's face hardened as Kate told him about the conversation she had heard between Cooney and Brady. At Lee's request, she gave him a close description of Brady.

'I'm mighty obliged for what you've just told me,' said Lee, when Kate had finished. 'I never believed that my mother would kill herself, or that my father would gamble his ranch away. My job now is to see that Cooney and Brady, as well as Maxwell, pay for what they've done.'

Kate explained how she and Alice had been virtual prisoners of Cooney since arriving in Bledsoe, and she asked Lee and Webster if they would help in getting her and Alice safely to Amarillo before Cooney could do anything to stop them. She said they would probably not be missed till the following morning.

Lee looked at Webster. 'You got any ideas, Mr Webster?' he asked.

Webster pondered for a moment before he replied.

'Can you ladies ride?' he asked.

Both the women nodded.

'Good,' he said. 'We'll get you on the next stage to Amarillo. But you won't get on here. The word would get to Cooney. You'd better join the stage at the next station south. It's a swing station, about twelve miles from here.

'The liveryman here in Bledsoe's a good friend of mine. He'll loan us a couple of horses. Then you can ride to the swing station. I'll give you a letter for the man who's running it. His name is Mark Carter. He happens to be a cousin of mine. The stage ain't usually full. With luck, there'll be a couple of seats left.'

'That's great,' said Kate, 'but there's just one problem. With Cooney keeping us short of money, we ain't got enough for the fare.'

'I'm taking care of that,' said Lee. 'You've helped me a lot. I'm going to ride with you to the swing station, to make sure you get there safe.'

The two women looked relieved.

'We're sure going to be glad,' said Kate, 'to see the last of Bledsoe and of Cooney's saloon. If he ever comes to trial, I'll be glad to testify against him.'

They left later in the night, arriving at the swing station well before the stage was due. Lee handed Webster's letter to Carter, the man in charge. He read it, then spoke to them.

'Come inside,' he said, 'and rest awhile. There's some coffee on the stove. There won't be no trouble getting the two ladies on the stage.'

When the stage rolled up, it was still dark. Carter had a few words with the driver before changing the team. Then he spoke to the two women.

'It's all right,' he said. 'You can get on board. You'll be leaving soon.'

Lee helped the women on to the coach, and waited till it moved off. Then, leaving with Carter the horses which had carried the two women, he rode back to Bledsoe. Unobserved, he rode to the rear of the store, tied his horse to a hitching rail, and entered the living-quarters.

THREE

It was ten o'clock in the morning, with Kate and Alice well on their way to Amarillo, when Mellor, the barkeep, went into Cooney's room and told him that the two saloon girls were nowhere to be found, and that their travelling bags and personal items were missing from their rooms.

Cooney cursed. 'Ask around,' he said, 'and find out if anybody's seen them.'

After forty minutes, Mellor returned. 'I've asked everywhere,' he said, 'and nobody's seen them. But I reckon I know how they got out of the saloon without anybody seeing or hearing them. There's a ladder lying in the alley under the veranda. The painter said he left it on the veranda when he finished work yesterday.'

'Somebody in town must know what's

happened to them,' said Cooney, fuming. 'I'm gong to collect some hands from the ranch, and we'll search every building in this town.'

Three hours later the search had been completed, with no sign of the missing women. Cooney then sent his men on a search of the surrounding area. During this, they interrogated Carter, the swing station manager, who told them that he'd seen no sign of the two women.

Vic Martin, the Circle D ramrod, reported back to Cooney at the saloon around midnight. He was a big man, mean-looking, with massive shoulders. He told Cooney that the search had proved fruitless.

'Somebody must have helped them get away,' said Cooney, 'but who?'

'They didn't know anything about the fake IOU and about how Vickery's wife really died, did they?' asked Martin.

'Don't see how they could,' Cooney replied. 'I know they've been wanting to quit for a while. They must have decided on taking a chance of getting away now. I'll get a couple more girls for the saloon as soon as I can.'

After taking breakfast Lee waited until the bank was open, then he walked along the street and went inside to see Maxwell, the manager. The bank was empty of customers. The teller, Bradley, took Lee to Maxwell's office.

The manager, sitting at his desk, looked up as Lee entered and stood facing him, on the other side of the desk. Looking at Lee's face, Maxwell felt a sudden premonition of trouble. The teller, on leaving them, left the office door very slightly ajar, and stood outside, listening. He, also, had sensed that trouble was in the air, and he was curious to hear the cause.

Inside the office, dispensing with any formalities, Lee spoke to the banker.

'I had a long talk with one of the saloon girls before she left town,' he said. 'She overheard a conversation in the saloon, and she's willing to give evidence before a court that, using a fake IOU and with your help, Cooney took over the Box V Ranch illegally.'

Maxwell's face paled visibly, as he stared at Lee.

'I don't know what you're talking about,' he said. His voice was strained, and his eyes avoided Lee's.

Outside the door, the teller heard the door from the street open and close as a customer came into the bank. He hesitated for a moment, then went back to the counter. As he reached it, the door opened again and another customer came in.

Inside the banker's office, Lee continued. 'There's no denying it, Maxwell,' he said. 'The question is, did you also have something to do with the murder of my mother?'

Maxwell started. 'Murder!' he said. 'I thought she'd shot herself.'

'Not so,' said Lee. 'The same saloon girl heard Cooney talking with the man he'd hired to do the job. I'm wondering just how much you knew about Cooney's plan to have my mother killed.'

Maxwell was visibly shaken. 'I knew nothing about it,' he shouted. 'I always believed that she took her own life.'

Lee was inclined to believe that the banker was telling the truth.

'Assuming that's true,' he said, 'you still have a lot of explaining to do.'

'All right,' said Maxwell, 'I did tell a lie about that IOU. I wrote it out myself. I copied your father's handwriting and signature from some documents I have in my files. Cooney forced me into it. He threatened, if I didn't do as he wanted, that he'd open up a new bank in town and force me out of business.'

'Forging that IOU was criminal,' said Lee, 'and you'll have to pay for it. I've got a feeling that you had nothing to do with my mother's murder. I'm going to see that Cooney and his hired killer pay for that.

'It's going to be a lot easier for me if Cooney doesn't know that I'm on to him. I've got to rely on you not to tell him that. I need time to work on a plan to get him before a judge. If you keep your mouth shut, I'll tell the law that you helped me to capture Cooney. Is it a deal?'

'It's a deal,' said the banker, hurriedly. 'I felt pretty bad about helping Cooney to steal the Box V.'

When Lee got back to the store, he told the Websters about Maxwell's confession. He said he was working on a plan which would bring Cooney and Brady before the law.

When the bank closed for an hour at noon, the teller hurried along to the saloon, where he found Cooney alone in his office.

'I've been watching Maxwell like you told me,' he said. 'Just after the bank opened, Vickery came in to see him in his office. I listened outside the door, and I heard Vickery say that one of your saloon girls was willing to give evidence that Maxwell had forged an IOU so that you could take over the Box V Ranch.

'I had to go back to the counter, because

two customers came in, so I didn't hear no more. Vickery left soon after.'

Shocked at the news, Cooney paid Bradley for the information, then sat alone in his office for a while, reviewing the situation, and wondering what Lee was planning to do next.

He was expecting his foreman to turn up at any time, and he waited in his room until Martin arrived. After a brief discussion the foreman left with instructions to report back to Cooney at the saloon at eight o'clock in the evening.

When Martin returned at the appointed time, he and Cooney walked to the small detached house on the edge of town where Maxwell lived alone. The street was deserted. Cooney knocked on the door, and when the banker opened it, he pushed his way inside, followed by Martin, who closed the door behind him as Cooney confronted Maxwell.

'I heard about the visit you had from Vickery this morning,' he said, 'and I know that one of the saloon girls has told him about the forged IOU. Just how she got to know about that, I can't figure out. What I want to know now is whether Vickery knows anything else, and why didn't you tell me about his visit?'

Maxwell tried to check a rising sense of panic. He guessed that the teller had been eavesdropping at his office door, but didn't know how much he had heard. Probably only Lee's accusation about the forged IOU. Cooney would have mentioned anything else.

'Vickery told me that he knew about me forging the IOU so that you could take the Box V over,' said Maxwell. His voice was shaking. 'He told me I'd have to pay for my part in the theft when he handed you over to the law.

'I told him that he was crazy. I said that I'd seen his father write out the IOU himself, and that you'd showed it to me later. Vickery then said he'd be back when he'd collected more evidence. Then he left.

44

'When you turned up here, I was just thinking I'd walk along to the saloon, to tell you all about it.'

'Seems to me you should have told me right away,' said Cooney. 'I reckon you and Vickery must have made a deal of some sort. I want the truth out of you, Maxwell, and I aim to get it.'

He made a sign to Martin, who advanced on the banker. Maxwell, fear showing on his face, retreated until his back was against the wall. Martin punched him hard on each side of his face in turn, then in the stomach. He grasped the banker by the shoulders, and threw him down to the floor. As Maxwell fell, his head slammed against a chest standing against the wall.

The banker lay stunned for a few moments. When he came to, he cringed back, seeing that Martin was raising his foot to kick him. He felt the toe of the ramrod's boot smash into his ribs, and screamed at the explosion of pain in his side. Martin raised his foot to strike again.

'All right! All right!' groaned Maxwell, cringing back against the wall, his face contorted with pain. 'I'll tell you.'

Haltingly, too scared to tell anything but the truth, the banker gave a full account of his conversation with Lee earlier in the day. When he had finished, he remained lying on the floor, holding one hand against the wound on his head, and the other against his ribs.

Cooney and Martin looked at one another. Then, leaving Maxwell lying on the floor, they walked to the other side of the room, out of earshot of the banker.

'It seems,' said Cooney, 'that Vickery knows the truth about his mother's death as well as about the IOU. We'll have to kill him. And we've got to get rid of Maxwell too. He knows too much.'

He walked over to the banker, and leaned over him. Without hesitation, and before Maxwell realized what was happening, Cooney drew his six-gun and shot the banker in the side of the head. Death was instantaneous. Cooney stood erect, then spoke to Martin.

'Clean up any blood you can see in here,' he said, 'then get another horse and take Maxwell out of town without anybody seeing you leave. Bury him some place where the body'll never be found. Then come back to my office around eight tomorrow morning.

'Seeing as it's Saturday tomorrow, maybe Maxwell won't be missed till Monday morning.'

As instructed, Martin returned to Cooney's office at the saloon on the following morning.

'Now that we know,' said Cooney, 'that Vickery knows all about the IOU and the way his mother died, we ain't got no choice but to get rid of him. It ain't a good idea to do it in town. If we could ambush him somewhere out of town, we could bury the body and nobody'd be any the wiser.

'But we'll have to do it quick. Remember, Maxwell said that Vickery was working on a plan to hand me over to the law. It's lucky that we have the advantage that Vickery don't know that we know he's on to us.'

'Just how do we get him out of town?' asked Martin.

Cooney pondered over the problem for a short while. Then he spoke to the ramrod.

'I have an idea,' he said. 'It might work.'

They discussed the rancher's plan for the next twenty minutes, then Martin prepared to leave.

'Before you go,' said Cooney, 'are you absolutely sure that the new ranch hand Baldwin ain't been seen yet by anybody in town?'

'I'm sure of it,' Martin replied.

'Then go out to the Box V at daybreak with him and two other hands, and do what's necessary. And make sure Baldwin knows exactly what to do when he rides into town later on.'

As Martin was moving towards the door, Cooney stopped him.

'Wait a minute,' he said. 'I've just decided to go back to the ranch with you. Now

Vickery knows what he does, I reckon I'll be safer out at the Circle D. You'd better put a couple of night guards out, just in case.'

At two hours after noon on the following day, the new Circle D ranch hand, Baldwin, rode into town from the Box V. A man with a criminal record, he had been recruited by Cooney on a recent visit he had made to Indian Territory.

Baldwin rode up to the store, tied his horse to the hitching rail, and went inside. He bought some tobacco and chatted with Webster for a while, telling the storekeeper that he was riding through, on his way to Amarillo.

He walked towards the door, then suddenly turned and walked back to the counter.

'There's something I meant to ask you about,' he said. 'Riding along the valley, I passed the Box V buildings, and a bit further on I climbed a knoll to see if I could see any sign of Bledsoe ahead.

'On the side of the knoll, I saw a couple of

graves, with crosses lying by them, both marked with the name Vickery. What I couldn't figure out was why the graves weren't filled in, with the crosses standing upright. I could see the tops of the coffins. I was wondering if you know anything about it.'

'I don't,' said Webster, bewildered by the news. 'The last time I was there, one of the graves was already filled in, and I watched the other one being filled after a burial. I'd be obliged if you'd wait here a minute.'

He went through to the living-quarters, and returned almost immediately with Lee.

'This is Mr Vickery,' he said. 'His parents were buried in the spot you've just been talking about. He'd be obliged if you'd tell him what you've just told me.'

When Baldwin had done this, Lee asked him if he had seen anybody around the Box V buildings.

'No, I didn't,' Baldwin replied. 'The place looked deserted to me. I knocked on the door of the house before I climbed the knoll, but nobody answered.'

Baldwin left shortly after, and Lee discussed the news with the storekeeper.

'If what that man says is true,' said Lee, 'it just don't make no sense. I've got to go out and see those graves for myself, and fill them in if that's needed. I'm leaving now.'

'Take care,' said Webster. 'Watch out for Circle D hands.'

'I'll do that,' said Lee, 'but I don't expect no trouble from Cooney just now. He doesn't know that I've learned the truth about what happened here. If you can spare me a shovel, I'll take it with me, in case I need it when I get there.'

FOUR

When Lee arrived close to the knoll, which lay between him and the house, he left his horse in a grove of trees off the trail, then approached the knoll on foot and climbed up to the graves. They were just as described by the stranger in the store.

Lee checked that the coffin lids had not been disturbed. Then he worked his way round the knoll until he had a good view, from cover, of the ranch buildings. A lone saddled horse was standing at the hitching rail close to the house, but there was no sign of its rider.

Lee lay watching for a while, but there was no sign of movement from below. He decided to confront the owner of the horse to see if he could solve the mystery of the disturbed graves.

He moved round to the graves, then climbed down to the foot of the knoll and started to circle it. As soon as the ranch house was in view, he bent almost double, and taking a path that afforded him a certain amount of cover, he ran up to the rear of the house.

He stood against the wall for a moment, then ran round the side of the house, ducking under the windows. Cautiously he turned the corner at the front, then he moved silently to the door. It was slightly ajar.

He paused for a moment, and drew his Colt .45 Peacemaker from its holster. Then he kicked the door open, and stepped inside. Immediately, he realized that he had fallen into a deadly trap.

Three of Cooney's men were standing inside the room. One, called Sinclair, was standing in the middle of the room, slightly to Lee's left. By his side was another hand called Brown, and the ramrod Martin was standing in a bedroom doorway in the far right-hand corner of the room. Each of the three men had a revolver in his hand.

Lee exploded into action. He dived down to his left, and before he hit the floor he fired at Sinclair, hitting him in the chest. As Lee hit the floor, he rolled over once, then fired at Brown, hitting him in the neck, before scrambling desperately to the side of a large armchair which sheltered him from Martin.

Lee had not escaped unscathed. Each of his three opponents had fired at him, and he had a bullet wound high on his chest, near the left shoulder, as well as one on his right leg. Martin's shot had narrowly missed its target, before burying itself in the floor. As Lee disappeared out of his view, Martin hurriedly stepped back inside the bedroom, and moved out of sight of Lee.

From his cover, Lee looked at Brown and Sinclair. He could see their guns lying on the floor beside them. Brown was lying motionless. As Lee's eyes moved to Sinclair, the wounded man tried to raise himself to a sitting position, then, with a groan which trailed off into silence, he slumped down, his head slopped sideways, and he lay motionless beside his partner. Lee suspected that both men were dead.

He decided to try and fool Martin. He took off his boots, then gave what he hoped was a realistic groan of intense pain, which he suddenly cut short. He held his six-gun up, then allowed it to drop with a clatter on to the bare floor. He jerked his two boots forward, so that the toes and heels were visible to Martin, peering out of the bedroom.

Leaving his boots in that position, Lee picked up his six-gun, and crawled painfully, and as silently as he could, round the back of the armchair and along the floor between the wall and the back of a large adjacent couch.

He stopped near the far end of the couch and lay flat on the floor, looking underneath the couch into the centre of the room. He lay there, silent and unmoving, trying to ignore the pains in his chest and leg, and waiting for Martin's next move.

Almost five minutes went by before he heard a slight sound, and saw the ramrod's feet come in view. Martin was slowly approaching the armchair against which he believed Lee to be lying. The boots had not moved since Martin had heard something which might, he thought, have been the sound of Lee's gun falling to the floor.

Lee saw that Martin had reached a point not far from the armchair. He knew that, in a moment, the ramrod would discover that there was no one behind it.

He sat up, then rose quickly behind the couch on his good leg, with the Peacemaker in his hand. Martin, concentrating on the armchair, saw Lee out of the corner of his eye, and frantically swung his six-gun round to bear on his opponent. But he was too late. The bullet from Lee's revolver struck him in the head before he had lined up and fired his own gun. He crashed to the floor on his back, and lay still.

Lee held on to the back of the couch for a few moments, until an attack of giddiness abated. Then he limped out from behind it, and took a look at the three men lying motionless on the floor. All three were dead.

He went over to a chair, and sat down on it while he looked at his wounds. The bullet which had struck him high on the chest was, he was sure, lodged in the wound, which was bleeding, and very painful. The injury on his leg had been caused by a bullet tearing through the flesh at the back of his leg, below the knee, before passing on. This wound, also, was bleeding, and walking was painful.

He found a pail in the kitchen, and walked down to the river to fill it with water. On his way, he looked inside the barn. As he expected, there were two saddled horses inside. Back in the house, he found a bedsheet in a cupboard; he used it to wash his wounds and bandage them as best he could.

When he had done this, he stood by the window, considering his next move. He knew that once the three dead men from the Circle D were found, the search for himself would be on, and he would not be safe in Bledsoe.

He decided to head for a town called Purdy, which Seth Webster had once mentioned. It lay about twenty-five miles to the south. With luck he would find a doctor there who would attend to his wounds.

As he was about to turn away from the window, to walk towards the door, a movement outside caught his attention. Four riders had just rounded the foot of the knoll, and were heading towards the house. Lee recognized the rider in the lead. It was Cooney.

Lee could not leave the house without being spotted by the Circle D riders and, in his present condition, a confrontation with Cooney and his men was, he figured, something which would almost certainly lead to his own death.

He limped into the bedroom and opened the long chest which he had looked into on a previous visit to the house. The two blankets he had seen then were still lying on the bottom of it.

He stepped into the chest, and lay down, face upwards, on the blankets. He lowered the lid and waited, his Peacemaker in his right hand. Both his wounds were causing him severe pain, and he was feeling weak from shock and the loss of blood.

He raised the lid of the chest just a fraction, and supported it in that position with a couple of coins from his pocket. A little later, he stiffened as he heard the sounds of men entering the house. Immediately after this came the sound of voices raised in anger, as the three bodies were discovered. Then Lee heard somebody come into the bedroom in which he was hiding.

The man who had entered the bedroom looked under the bed, and into the two clothes' cupboards. Then his eye fell on the chest, and he walked up to it. He was reaching out to lift up the lid when Cooney called out to him from the living-room. He ran out of the bedroom and joined the rancher and the other two hands.

'Vickery's left the house,' said Cooney, pointing to the trail of blood-spots leading through the doorway to the outside, and it looks like he's hurt bad.

'It'll be dark soon. First, we'll search the ranch buildings for Vickery. If we don't find him, you three ride to Bledsoe, in case he's gone back there. Search the place thoroughly, then go back to the Circle D. If you've found him, bring him with you. I'm going back there now. I'll send some men out here to pick up the bodies.'

In the bedroom, Lee heard the faint sounds of voices for a while. Then came the sound of a door being slammed. After that there was silence. He waited for half an hour, then pushed up the lid of the chest and eased himself out. He stood listening in the bedroom for a short while, then limped into the living-room. The three dead men were still lying on the floor.

Looking out through the window, he

could see no sign of Cooney and his men, but he expected that a buckboard would be coming along soon to collect the bodies. He left the house and made his way to the grove in which he had left his horse. It was still there. He put his foot in the stirrup and groaned with pain as he pulled himself up into the saddle. In the growing darkness, he headed slowly across the valley, in a southerly direction.

As his mount climbed out of the valley, Lee was struck by a sudden attack of faintness, and he had to will himself to stay in the saddle. He left the valley and carried on doggedly, slumped forward in the saddle, occasionally looking backwards to check that the North Star was still directly behind him. As time went by, the pace of his mount grew slower and slower, and it started to drift off the southerly course which Lee had followed earlier during the ride.

For long spells, he was only semi-conscious. He had no idea of how long he had been riding, or of how far he had come, but he forced himself to stay in the saddle until, just as dawn was breaking, he lost consciousness and fell sideways off his horse. As he hit the hard ground, his head slammed against it, and he lay there motionless.

Two hours later, in the ranch house of the small Crazy R ranch, two miles north-west of the position where Lee was lying unconscious, Miriam Randle was preparing to leave on the buckboard, to pick up some supplies in Purdy, six miles to the southeast.

Miriam was the daughter of rancher Pete Randle and his wife Mary. She was a slim, attractive, raven-haired girl in her early twenties, with no shortage of male admirers in the area.

She checked the list of supplies with her parents, then left the house and climbed up on the buckboard, to which two horses had already been hitched by a ranch hand. She drove away from the ranch buildings and on to the trail leading to Purdy.

As she joined the trail, the ranch foreman

Wes Tucker rode up to the buckboard from behind, then continued along by her side. He was heading out on to the range to take a look at some sick cows that a hand had noticed just before dark on the previous day, not far off the trail to Purdy.

Tucker, in his fifties, was an old friend of Pete Randle, from the days before Randle had become a rancher, and Miriam's father trusted him implicitly. Miriam looked on him as an uncle, rather than a hired hand. They chatted for a while, then Tucker pointed to a ridge ahead of them, on the left.

'I'm going to take a look at the cattle on the other side of that ridge,' he said, then veered off to the left.

Miriam carried on in the direction of Purdy. Just over a mile after parting company with the foreman, she spotted a saddled horse grazing ahead, just off the trail. Looking round for the rider, she saw, not far from the horse, something lying on the ground.

She left the trail and headed towards it. As

she drew closer, she could see the motionless figure of a man lying on the ground. She drove on a little further, then stopped the buckboard, climbed down, and ran over to look at him.

As she turned him over on to his back, she could see that he was a stranger. From the bloodstained clothing, she guessed that there were wounds on his leg and chest, and she could see a cut and bruise on his temple. His eyes were closed. She spoke to him, but there was no response. She patted his face, and spoke again.

Lee's eyes opened, and focused on the face of the girl leaning over him.

'I can see you're hurt bad,' said Miriam. 'Can you climb on the buckboard?'

'I'll try,' said Lee, faintly. He slowly sat up, then started to rise to his feet, but almost immediately he collapsed on to the ground, and lay there, with his eyes closed.

Miriam, remembering that Tucker was not that far away, ran for the rifle under the seat of the buckboard. Her father insisted that she always took the weapon with her when driving the buckboard alone.

Picking up the rifle, she fired three evenly spaced shots in the air, then ran back to the wounded man and knelt down beside him. She saw that his eyes were open again.

'We should be getting some help soon,' she said. 'What's your name?'

'Lee Vickery,' replied Lee, weakly.

They did not have long to wait before Miriam saw Wes Tucker, riding at full stretch over a low ridge in the distance, and heading in their direction. Minutes later, he reached them, dismounted, and ran over to Miriam, still kneeling by Lee. Relieved, he saw that she was unharmed.

'You sure had me worried, Miriam,' he said. 'I figured you were in trouble.'

'It's Mr Vickery here that's in trouble,' said Miriam.

'I found him lying here. That must be his horse over there. It looks like he's hurt bad.'

'It sure does,' said the foreman, taking a look at Lee's wounds. 'He needs a doctor.'

'If we can get him on to the buckboard,' said Miriam, 'I'll take him back to the ranch while you ride to Purdy and get Doc Sawyer to come out and see him.'

'Right,' said Tucker. The two of them helped Lee on to the buckboard. Tucker tied Lee's horse behind it, then rode off towards Purdy. Miriam turned the buckboard, and headed for the Crazy R ranch house.

Mary Randle, looking through a ranch house window, saw the buckboard approaching. She called her husband, and they both went outside, curious about Miriam's early return and the saddled horse trailing behind the buckboard. When Miriam stopped outside the house, they could see Lee lying on the floor of the buckboard.

'I found this man lying out on the range,' said Miriam. 'He has a couple of gunshot wounds and a sore head. Wes has gone to Purdy for the doctor. Meanwhile, we'd better get him inside.'

Mary Randle ran inside to get a bed ready, and the rancher called a couple of hands over to carry Lee into the house and lay him down on the bed. The two women took off his vest and shirt, and cut along the leg of his pants to reveal the wound on the back of his leg.

They set about washing off the blood, and cleansing the wounds as best they could. They put temporary bandages on to cover the wounds until the doctor arrived.

'There's a bullet inside his chest,' said Mary Randle, speaking to her daughter in the living-room. 'Did he tell you anything about himself?'

'Only that his name's Lee Vickery,' Miriam replied. 'Then he blacked out. I reckon we'll have to wait a while before we find out from him just how he came to be in such a fix.'

FIVE

It was half an hour before noon when the doctor turned up at the ranch house with Tucker. Doc Sawyer was a short, rotund man, kindly and pleasant in manner. He was well-respected in the community. Miriam led him to the bedroom where Lee was lying, drifting in and out of consciousness. Her mother and father, standing by the bed, greeted Sawyer, then went into the living-room. Miriam remained.

The doctor removed the bandages, and closely inspected the wounds on the leg and chest.

'The wound on the leg should heal all right, once it's properly cleaned up,' he said, 'but there's a bullet inside the wound on the top of the chest. I'll have to take it out.'

He called Miriam's father in to help hold

the patient steady, then he probed inside the wound. Lee groaned as he felt the searing pain resulting from this procedure. Eventually, Sawyer succeeded in extracting the bullet. He showed it to Randle and his daughter.

'I don't think,' he said, 'that this bullet's done any serious damage, but this man's going to be laid up for a spell. Can he stay here till we find out more about him?'

'Of course,' said Mary Randle.

The doctor cleaned and bandaged the wounds, including the cut on the temple. Then he stood looking down at his patient.

'A good-looking man,' he said. 'I'm as curious as you are about where he's from, and how he got those wounds. I suppose he could be on the run from the law, but he sure don't look like a criminal to me. I'll come out tomorrow to see how he's getting on.'

He leaned over as his patient feebly gestured to him, then listened as Lee spoke to him in a barely audible voice, before lying still once again, with his eyes closed.

'He asked me,' said Sawyer to Miriam and her father, 'not to tell anybody in town about him being here. I've got a feeling he's in danger from somebody, but not from the law, so I'm going to do as he asks. Likely you'll do the same?'

Randle nodded. 'We'll keep quiet,' he said.

The women tended to Lee for the rest of the day, and kept an eye on him overnight. When morning came, his head was clear, and he was able to tell the Randles, haltingly, how he came to be lying, wounded, on the Crazy R range. He told his listeners of Cooney's part in the death of his mother, and of his takeover of the Box V Ranch.

'This man Cooney,' said Randle, 'd'you reckon he'll be looking for you?'

'I'm sure of it,' Lee replied, 'which is why I ain't happy about staying here. I figure I should move on, in case Cooney finds out that you've taken me in. Maybe he'll cause you trouble.'

'I ain't worried about that,' said Randle,

'not with my men around. You're welcome to stay here till you're fit to leave. When that time comes, are you figuring on going after this man Cooney?'

'I am,' Lee replied. 'I'm going to hand him over to the law. I've got a witness who'll testify against him.'

Miriam brought Lee some food and drink at midday, and stayed chatting with him for a while. He told her of his spell as a peace officer in Kansas, and she recounted how she and her parents had moved westward from Missouri by covered wagon, and had eventually settled in the Panhandle, where her father used their savings to establish the Crazy R.

Lee felt strongly attracted to the girl, and was grateful to her and her parents. When she left him, he fell into a deep sleep, and did not wake until Doc Sawyer arrived to see him three hours later. Randle met the doctor outside, and repeated to him what Lee had told them earlier in the day.

Then Sawyer went inside, and Miriam and

her father watched as he took a look at Lee's wounds, then renewed the bandages.

'Everything's fine,' he told Lee. 'No sign of infection so far.'

He paused, then continued: 'You'll be interested to hear,' he said, 'that a couple of tough-looking characters rode into town this morning, and started asking if anybody had seen you around. They gave a good description of you. They said they were bounty hunters, and you were wanted by the law, but they didn't have a WANTED notice to show around.

'Seeing as I was the only person in town who knew you were at the Crazy R, they drew a blank, and left town around midday.'

'I'm obliged to you,' said Lee.

'I'll call and see you in a couple of days,' said Sawyer. 'Meanwhile, stay in bed.'

During the next two and a half weeks there were no further enquiries about sightings of Lee in the area, and his condition rapidly improved, so much so, that at the end of that period he asked Miriam if he could accompany her on the buckboard into town, in order to make some purchases at the store.

'Sure,' she said. 'If you're up to it. I'll be glad of the company. We'll go this morning if you like, as soon as you're ready.'

Half an hour later, Lee buckled on his gunbelt, and helped Miriam hitch two horses to the buckboard. Then, with Miriam holding the reins, and Lee seated by her side, they headed in the direction of Purdy, chatting as they moved along.

They had covered two and a half miles, when Lee spotted a lone rider angling towards them from the north. Miriam saw him at the same time.

'Looks like a stranger,' she said, and Lee rested his hand on the butt of his Peace-maker.

A few minutes later, the rider came up alongside, and Miriam brought the buck-board to a halt.

The two men recognized each other at the same instant.

'Steve!' said Lee.

'Damn me, if it ain't Lee,' said the rider, an amiable-looking man, of similar build to Lee, and around the same age. He was clean-shaven, and his hair was dark.

Lee turned to Miriam. 'This is Steve Norton, Miriam,' he said. 'He's an old friend and partner of mine. We were deputy sheriffs together in Kansas.'

Steve shook hands with Miriam, then rode his horse close to Lee, as the buckboard moved on, towards Purdy.

'Where are you heading, Steve?' asked Lee.

'Purdy,' Steve replied. 'I'm figuring to stay the night there. When I saw the buckboard, I was aiming to ask the driver if I was anywhere near the place.'

'We're on our way there,' said Lee. 'It's three or four miles from here. Have you quit the deputy sheriff's job in Kansas?'

Steve nodded. 'About a month ago,' he said. 'I got a hankering to take a look at the Panhandle, and maybe New Mexico and Colorado. But how about yourself? You ain't looking too good. Don't your father run a spread north of here?'

'He did,' replied Lee, grimly, and proceeded to tell his friend about the deaths of his parents, the takeover of the Box V by Cooney, and subsequent events.

'That's quite a story,' said Steve, 'and I'm mighty sorry to hear about your folks. What're you aiming to do when you're fit again?'

'Go after Cooney, of course,' Lee replied, 'and then Brady.'

'It seems to me,' said his friend, 'that you could do with some help. And I'm just the man for the job. To tell the truth, I've been a mite bored for the last few weeks. What I badly need is some action.'

Lee turned to look at his friend. 'You sure?' he asked. 'Cooney ain't short of gunslingers to do his dirty work for him.'

'I'm sure,' said Steve. 'When d'you plan to leave here?'

'The doc says the day after tomorrow should see me fit to ride,' said Lee, 'and I'm

76

sure going to be a lot happier with you riding with me.'

'Somebody's got to look after you,' grinned Steve. 'I'll stay on in town till you're ready to go.'

When they reached Purdy, and stopped outside the general store, Steve rode on to the blacksmith shop, after arranging to see his friend again before Lee left for the Crazy R.

Inside the store Lee made a few small purchases from the storekeeper's wife, while the storekeeper attended to Miriam. Then he went out on to the boardwalk, and stood there, looking along the street. Two riders were coming into town from the north-west.

Lee observed them as they passed him. He was sure that they were neither townsmen, nor ordinary cowhands or settlers. They both wore six-guns, and there was a faintly menacing air about them. He wondered for a moment whether they were Cooney's men, still searching for him, but they both glanced at him and showed no interest.

One of the riders, the nearest to Lee, had red hair and a deep scar on his right cheek. He was riding a handsome palomino. Both men were bearded and travel-stained.

As his eyes followed them along the street, Lee saw Steve come out of the blacksmith shop and walk further along the street towards the livery stable. Suddenly, the red-haired rider stopped, called out something to his companion, and pointed towards Steve's back. The other rider reined his horse in, and both men watched Steve as he went into the livery stable.

Curious, Lee continued to watch the two riders, as they spoke hurriedly to one another, then looked towards the building across the street from the livery stable. It was a building badly in need of repair, and obviously not in use. A faded sign above the door indicated that it had, at one time, been a dry-goods store.

The two men rode off the street towards the rear of the building, passing out of Lee's view. Lee ran round to the back of the store, then along the backs of the buildings lining the street, until he reached the rear of the livery stable, where he saw an open door.

He went inside, and found Steve talking to Jarvis the liveryman. Surprised, Steve broke off the conversation as Lee ran towards him.

'Two armed men just rode into town, Steve,' he said, 'and they looked mighty interested when they spotted you walking towards the stable. They rode their horses to the back of what used to be the dry-goods store directly opposite the stable, on the other side of the Street. The way they were acting, I've got a strong feeling they're in that building now, waiting to gun you down as soon as you leave here.'

He turned to Jarvis. 'Is it easy to get into that building from the back?' he asked.

'I reckon so,' Jarvis replied. 'The last time I was round there, I noticed that a hinge had broken on the back door, and it was jammed half-open.'

'You've always had a good nose for trouble, Lee,' said Steve, 'so I'm taking heed of what you say. But I can't think who those two might be.'

'I got a pretty good look at one of them,' said Lee. 'He was a red-haired, bearded man, medium height, with a scarred cheek. He was riding a big palomino.'

Steve closed his eyes and pondered, but only for a moment. Then his eyes snapped open.

'So that's it,' he said. 'The man you've just described sounds very much like Morg Barclay. His brother Ned was the leader of an outlaw gang we were chasing in Kansas not long before I quit my job as deputy sheriff.

'We had a shoot-out with the gang, and I shot Ned Barclay. He died soon after. It could be that Morg's looking for revenge. I guess the man with him is Tom Tracy. They're both bounty hunters, and by all accounts they're expert at the job.

'I've heard it said that their guns are for hire to anybody with the right kind of money who wants a dirty job done. And that includes murder. But the law ain't been able to catch up with them yet.'

'How d'you want to play this, Steve?' asked Lee.

'Let's have a go at sneaking up behind them and taking their guns,' said Steve. 'Maybe, with you helping me, we can persuade them it ain't a good idea to go after a lawman who was only doing his job.'

After Jarvis, at Steve's request, had described the interior of the abandoned building, Lee and Steve left by the rear door of the stable and ran along the backs of the buildings until they could cross the street without the risk of being seen by Barclay and Tracy. Running behind the buildings, they approached the back of the one in which they believed that the two men were waiting in ambush.

Slowing down as they drew near, they could see two horses standing behind the building, but there was no sign of their riders. The door into the building was standing half-open. Holding their revolvers,

Lee and Steve slipped silently through the doorway, and tiptoed quietly across the room to the door which led to the room at the front of the house in which the dry goods had previously been stored. The door was half-open.

As they peeped through the opening into the room beyond, they saw Barclay and Tracy standing at the big window facing the street, their gaze fixed on the entrance to the livery stable. Barclay was holding a six-gun, Tracy a rifle.

Lee and Steve moved silently through the doorway, and approached the two men from behind, taking advantage of the noisy passage of a large freight wagon along the street outside. Their intention was to get close enough to the two men so as to stun them by pistol-whipping them over the back of the head.

Lee moved towards Tracy, Steve towards Barclay. But as the wagon receded, a floor-board half-way across the room groaned as Steve stepped on it, and both Barclay and

Tracy whipped round, raising their weapons as they did so.

Barclay recognized Steve, and immediately fired at the man in front of him. But Steve had fired first, hitting Barclay in the chest. The slug from his opponent's six-gun passed harmlessly by Steve's right ear.

Tracy's reaction was slower than that of his partner, and at close quarters the rifle was not so easy to handle as a six-gun. Lee picked his target, and shot Tracy in the upper right arm before his opponent could fire. Tracy's rifle fell from his hand to the floor, against Barclay, who had collapsed and was lying motionless.

Lee stepped up to Tracy, and took his six-gun from the holster. Steve bent down to look at Barclay.

'He's cashed in,' he said. 'It's a pity he turned before I got close enough to pistol-whip him. It sure looked like they were waiting to ambush me.'

'What do we do with Tracy?' asked Lee.

'It all depends,' Steve replied. 'Let's take a

look at that arm.'

He walked up to the wounded man, and found the bullet-hole in the sleeve of his vest. With his knife, he cut open the vest sleeve, and took a close look at the wound.

'You're a lucky man, Tracy,' he said. 'There's no bullet in there. All you've got is a flesh wound. Just hold your hand over it for the time being, while you tell me how long you've been trailing me.'

'You ain't going to believe this,' said Tracy, hoarsely, 'but we ain't been trailing you. Morg just happened to spot you when we rode into town, and he just went plumb crazy. He figured this was a good chance to get even with you for killing his brother.'

'That sounds like a mighty tall story to me,' said Steve, 'but if it's true, what are you doing here in Purdy?'

'We were on our way to Bledsoe,' said Tracy, 'to see a rancher called Cooney. We ain't never met or heard of him before, but he got to hear of us somehow. He sent us a message saying he knew of our reputation, and that there was a job he wanted us to do. He said to come quick, and name our own price. Somebody must have told him where to send that message, but I ain't got no idea who that somebody was.'

Lee and Steve exchanged glances as Tracy paused for a moment, before continuing:

'Maybe I can prove that what I say is true,' he said. 'Look inside Morg's vest pocket. There should be a telegraph message in there.'

Steve bent over and took a folded sheet of paper from the dead man's pocket. He unfolded it and looked at the message on it. It was addressed to Morg Barclay, and confirmed what Tracy had just said. He handed the paper to Lee.

'Looks like he's telling the truth,' said Lee, when he had read the message. 'What do we do with him?'

'We could hand him over to the law for attempted murder,' said Steve, 'but that would take time that we need for other things right now. I reckon we can let him go,

85

provided that he forgets about going to see Cooney, and heads straight back to Kansas. One thing's sure. We don't want him in the Panhandle.'

'If he don't want to leave for Kansas, we'll get a few of the townspeople here to guard him till the law comes along. What's it going to be, Tracy?'

Tracy scowled. 'I ain't got much choice, do I?' he said. 'I'll head for Kansas.'

Lee and Tracy took him outside, then on to the street, where Jarvis and several other townspeople had gathered. Lee told them what had happened, and Jarvis said he would arrange for Barclay's body to be removed and buried.

Doc Sawyer, who was among the small group that had gathered on the street, took Tracy back to his house to attend to his wound. Steve and Lee accompanied them. When the wound had been cleaned and bandaged they went with Tracy to collect his horse, and escorted him to the eastern edge of town.

'Remember,' said Steve. 'Come back this way, and you're in real trouble.'

The two friends watched Tracy in silence as he rode off to the east.

SIX

When Lee and Steve returned to the store, Miriam was waiting on the boardwalk.

'Mr Jarvis told me what happened,' she said. 'Are you both all right?'

'We're both fine,' Lee replied. 'It's a pity a man had to die, but he brought it on himself. Like you heard, he was aiming to kill Steve here.'

'Are you ready to go back to the ranch?' she asked.

'I'm ready,' replied Lee. 'What're you aiming to do, Steve?'

'I'll stay in town today,' Steve replied. 'Tomorrow, I'll ride out to the Crazy R, and we'll have a talk about how we're going to deal with Cooney.'

On the way back to the ranch, Miriam was silent for a while. Then she asked Lee if the mission against Cooney was likely to be a dangerous one.

'There's always a risk when you're going up against a powerful, ruthless man like Cooney,' said Lee, 'but now that I've got Steve with me, I reckon that we can get the better of him. And when it's all over, the first thing I'm going to do is ride out here to see you, if that's something you'd like me to do.'

'It's something I'd like,' said Miriam, 'and I'm praying it won't be too long before you finish doing what you have to do, and come back safe.'

The following morning, Steve rode out to the ranch, and sat with Lee in the living-room.

'I've got a plan,' said Steve.

'I knew you had,' said Lee, 'as soon as I heard you tell Tracy he could go free, provided he rode straight back to Kansas. You aim to go to the Circle D and pass yourself off as Morg Barclay, don't you?'

Steve nodded. 'Seems like a good idea to me,' he said.

'I'm not so sure,' said Lee. 'If he happens to find out that you ain't who you say you are, you'll be lucky to get away alive.'

'I'd like to do it,' said Steve. 'I ain't forgotten the times you've risked your life for me when we were lawmen riding together in Kansas.'

'If you're set on doing it,' said Lee, 'it sure would help to have somebody in the enemy camp. It'd make it a lot easier to get our hands on Cooney. We'll ride north tomorrow, and look out for a place near the Circle D where I can hide out for the time being. Then you can ride on to the Circle D, and I'll pay a visit to the Websters, in Bledsoe, after dark.

'They were good friends of my parents. I'll tell them about our plan, and if you want to pass a message on to me, make an excuse to ride into town, and give the message to the Websters. I'll call in and see them each evening if I can. I'll be waiting to hear from you about the situation out at the Circle D.'

Steve returned to Purdy, then rode out to

the Crazy R the next morning to join Lee, who thanked the Randles for their help before the two friends rode off to the north.

Later in the day, about six miles south of the valley in which the Circle D was located, they investigated a small, secluded ravine, well off the trail.

'This'll do,' said Lee. 'I'll hide out here for the time being, and ride in to see the Websters after dark. Before you head for the Circle D, let's leave the horses here, and climb up the side of the ravine.'

When they had reached the top, Lee looked around, using the field glasses he was carrying with him. Seeing a small grove of trees in the distance, he pointed this out to Steve, and handed him the glasses.

'Remember exactly where that grove is, Steve,' he said. 'I've got a feeling it might come in useful if you get into trouble at the Circle D. After you've gone, I'm going to ride over there to take a look at it.'

After a further short conversation, Steve prepared to leave.

'I'll head straight for the Circle D,' he said, 'and find out Cooney's reason for sending for Barclay and Tracy. Then I'll make an excuse for riding into town.'

The two men parted company, and an hour later, Steve was approaching the Circle D ranch house. Two men were standing outside it, looking in his direction. As he drew closer, Steve was sure, from Lee's description, that one of them was Cooney, the owner of the Circle D. He rode up to the two men, and stopped in front of them.

'Mr Cooney?' he asked.

'That's me,' said Cooney curtly. 'What's your business here?'

'I'm Barclay,' said Steve, 'Morg Barclay. I got your message. Came here as soon as I could.'

He took the telegraph message from his pocket, bent down, and handed it to Cooney. The rancher looked at it, then gave some instructions to the man by his side. The man walked away. Cooney turned to Steve, who had dismounted.

'I was expecting two of you,' he said. 'Where's your partner?'

'He took sick the day I got your message,' Steve replied, 'and it looked like he'd be laid up for quite a while. So I figured I'd better come on my own.'

'Come inside,' said Cooney, 'and I'll tell you about the job I want you to do for me.'

Steve followed the rancher into the living-room, where they both sat down. Cooney told Steve about the two saloon girls who had escaped, and about his failed attempt to get rid of Lee, culminating in Lee's disappearance.

'I've got a new ramrod, Lassiter,' he said, 'on account of my old ramrod, Martin, being killed by Vickery. Lassiter knew of you in Kansas, and he recommended you for the job I want done. He ain't here just now. He left before you turned up. He's riding south to buy some cows for me. I reckon he'll be away nine or ten days.

'I've got a feeling that Vickery's hanging around somewhere nearby. I want you to

94

track him down and kill him.'

'Right,' said Steve, greatly relieved that Lassiter was temporarily away from the ranch. 'What does this Vickery look like?'

Cooney gave a detailed description of Lee. When he had done this, he told Steve what else he wanted him to do.

'After you've dealt with Vickery,' he said, 'I want you to find the two saloon girls, Alice and Kate. I'm near certain you'll find them in Amarillo. I want them both dead.'

He described the two girls, and gave the name of the saloon in Amarillo from which he had enticed them.

'This is going to cost you,' said Steve.

Cooney nodded. 'Whatever it takes,' he said.

'I'll ride into town in the morning,' said Steve. 'There's a few things I want from the store. Then I'll start on the search for Vickery. A good starting-point might be the place where he was wounded.'

'All right,' said Cooney. 'It goes without saying that the sooner you take care of Vickery, the better I'll be pleased. Supper'll be ready in an hour, in the cookshack, and you can use that cabin next to the bunkhouse while you're here.'

Steve walked his horse over to the cabin. He took off the saddle, and led his mount to the pasture enclosure nearby. On his way back to the cabin he studied the layout of the ranch buildings.

Inside the small cabin were two bunks. Steve lay down on one of them, and reviewed the situation. Now that Cooney had accepted him as Morg Barclay, he needed to work out a plan which would enable him and Lee to capture Cooney at a time when only a few of his men were available to help him. Once captured, he would be taken to Amarillo for trial.

When he heard the cook's call for supper, Steve went to the cookshack. He sat down at the long table, with fifteen ranch hands. Looking round, and listening to the conversation, it was clear to him that the men were not ordinary cowhands. There was a hardbitten look about them, and he guessed that they had been specially recruited by Cooney, not only to look after the cows, but also to help him in any nefarious activities he had in mind.

Nobody tried to engage Steve in conversation, and he guessed that the men knew of Barclay's reputation, and of Clooney's reason for wanting to hire him.

On that same evening, Lee rode from the ravine to Bledsoe, and left his horse on the outskirts of town. Keeping off the main street, he cautiously made his way to the rear of the store, watching for any sign that it was under surveillance. There was none. The store was closed, and a light was showing from the living-quarters at the rear.

Lee knocked on the door, which was opened by Abigail Webster. Open-mouthed, she stared at Lee, then quickly beckoned him inside and closed the door behind him. She led him into the living-room, where her husband was seated in an armchair.

'Glory be!' said Webster, as Lee came into view. 'We were just beginning to figure you were dead.'

Lee sat down and told the Websters of his gun-battle with Cooney's men at the Box V, and of his subsequent escape, wounded, followed by his encounter with his old friend Steve.

Webster told Lee that the town had twice been thoroughly searched for him by Cooney's men after his disappearance, and that Circle D hands had scoured the area for him for several days. The story put out by Cooney was that Lee had ambushed and murdered three of his hands, before disappearing.

Webster said that he and his wife had suspected that, for a few days after Lee's disappearance, Cooney had had the store watched after dark by an odd-job man called Hoskins, who worked in the saloon. They suspected that he was watching out for Lee from an empty, derelict shack behind the store.

'I remember Hoskins,' said Lee. 'A short man, lame in one leg.'

Lee told the Websters that Steve was at the Circle D, masquerading as Morg Barclay, and that he would be leaving a message for him at the store on the following day. Then he rode back to the ravine, after telling the storekeeper that he would ride in again to see them on the following evening.

On his way south, the Circle D ramrod, Lassiter, passed close by a homestead four miles east of Purdy. It was an hour before nightfall. The homesteader, working in a field close to the trail, waved to him, and Lassiter swung off the trail and approached him. He asked Preston, the homesteader, for water for himself and his horse. Preston led him to a well near the house. When the thirst of his mount and himself had been quenched, Lassiter thanked the homesteader, and prepared to ride on. Then a thought struck him. He spoke to Preston.

'I'm looking for a friend of mine called

Vickery,' he said. 'I have an idea that maybe he's somewhere in this area. I'm wondering if you've seen him.'

He went on to give a detailed description of Lee, whom he had seen in Bledsoe soon after Lee's first arrival there.

'As a matter of fact, I have seen him,' said Preston. 'He was in Purdy a few days ago. He was with another man who'd killed a man in town in a gun-battle. I don't know the name of the dead man.

'I was in town again this morning, and I heard that they had both left the area, heading north. Another thing I heard was that Vickery first turned up here about three weeks ago, with a couple of gunshot wounds.'

'Could you describe the man who was with my friend?' asked Lassiter.

'Sure,' said Preston. 'His name was Norton.' He went on to give Lassiter a good description of Steve.

Lassiter rode off the homestead. As he reached the trail outside, he hesitated. He was strongly tempted to ride into Purdy, to learn more about the gunfight and Lee Vickery's activities in town. But he decided that what he had just heard about Vickery was of sufficient importance to justify his immediate return to the Circle D, to pass the information on to Cooney. He turned his horse, and headed north.

Lassiter took only a few hours' rest during the night, and he arrived back at the Circle D at daybreak. He went straight to the ranch house and roused Cooney, who joined him in the living-room, wondering what urgent reason could have brought the ramrod back before his mission was completed.

Lassiter told Cooney that Vickery and a man called Norton had left the Purdy area recently, heading north.

'I wonder where they were aiming to hang out,' said Cooney. 'Vickery was pretty thick with the Websters at the store. Maybe he'll pay them a visit after dark. Send a man into town after breakfast, to tell Hoskins to keep an eye on the store, in case Vickery turns up there.

'Meantime, I'd better let Barclay know about Vickery before he leaves for town.'

'Barclay's here, then?' asked Lassiter.

Cooney nodded. 'He turned up not long after you left, but without his partner, Tracy. It seems that Tracy took sick, and had to stay behind.'

Hearing the sound of the cook's call to the hands to come to breakfast, Cooney moved to a window overlooking the entrance to the cookshack. Lassiter followed him. Cooney saw Steve come out of his cabin, and walk towards the cookshack. Several hands left the bunkhouse at the same time, and headed in the same direction.

'There's Barclay,' said Cooney, pointing.

Lassiter looked at the men heading for the cookshack.

'I can't see him,' he said.

'There,' said Cooney, pointing again. 'He's just passing the wood-pile.'

'That ain't Barclay!' said Lassiter.

Startled, Cooney turned to his foreman. 'You sure of that?' he asked.

'Dead sure,' Lassiter replied, 'but he sure fits the description of the man Norton, who was in Purdy with Vickery.'

'What in blazes is going on?' asked Cooney. 'We'd better find out pronto. We'll take Norton, if that's who he is, when he gets back to his cabin after breakfast. Get hold of Cowley. He can come to the cabin with us. I'm wondering what's happened to the real Morg Barclay.'

Thirty-five minutes later, Steve walked back to his cabin to pick up his gunbelt before riding into Bledsoe. Entering the cabin, he stopped abruptly as he faced three men, each of them holding a six-gun in his hand.

'You're out of luck, Norton,' said Cooney. 'Lassiter here is the only man in this outfit who knows Morg Barclay, and he's turned up unexpected-like. What I aim to find out from you is where we can find your friend Vickery. And don't be too long about it. I ain't a patient man.'

Steve, wondering how Cooney knew both his name, and the fact that he and Lee had teamed up, stayed silent.

'Looks like we're going to have to beat it out of him,' said Cooney. 'Get some rope, Cowley.'

The ranch hand returned shortly after with some pieces of rope. Following Cooney's instructions, he and the ramrod tied Steve's hands behind him. Then they put several turns of rope around his chest, under the armpits, and suspended him from a roof beam. His feet were just clear of the floor, and his back was against the wall. Last of all, they tied his feet together.

'Let me tell you, Norton,' said Cooney, 'that Cowley here fancies himself as a fist-fighter, and he's going to do his best to loosen your tongue. When you're ready to talk, just sing out.'

Cowley, a big, strong man, stepped up to Steve, and delivered two powerful punches to his left jaw. Steve rode them as best he could, but they left him half-dazed, and opened up a cut on his left cheek, which started bleeding.

'You got anything to say yet?' asked Cooney, 'like where we can find Vickery.'

Steve made no reply.

'Carry on, Cowley,' said Cooney.

Cowley threw a series of solid punches at the hapless prisoner, targeting the ribs and the midriff. He paused after each couple of blows, to give Steve a chance to speak, but the prisoner, his face distorted with pain, remained silent.

Breathing heavily, Cowley delivered two more heavy punches to Steve's jaw, and the prisoner's head slumped forward as he lost consciousness. Blood was dropping from his cheek.

Cooney and the others waited until Steve regained consciousness and lifted his head to look at them. Cowley raised his fists, ready to resume the attack.

Steve cringed. 'No, no!' he shouted. 'That's enough!' Some blood trickled from his mouth, and his voice shook as he continued. 'Near the trail that leads from Bledsoe to Purdy, a few miles south of the valley, there's a big rock outcrop. Half a mile south of that, there's a grove of trees. Vickery's hiding in there.'

'And just what are you doing here, pretending to be Barclay?' asked Cooney.

Steve remained silent. Cowley raised his fists again.

'All right, all right!' said Steve, weakly. 'I knew Vickery in Kansas, and I ran into him in Purdy. When Morg Barclay rode into town and saw me, he figured on taking revenge, because I'd killed his brother a while back. So I had to kill him. Vickery and me, we found that telegraph message from you in his pocket.'

Steve paused for a moment, then, haltingly, he continued.

'Vickery offered me money to come here and pass myself off as Morg Barclay. He wanted me to find out how many men you had here, and how much time you spent here yourself. And he wanted to know about the layout of the rooms inside the ranch house, and what sort of routine the ranch hands followed.

'I don't know why he wanted the information. He didn't tell me. But I guessed he was after you. The arrangement was that when I had the information he wanted, I'd ride out to the grove and pass it on to him. Then I'd leave the valley, and head for Kansas.'

'What happened to Tracy?' asked Cooney.

'He got hit in the arm during the fight I had with Barclay,' Steve replied. 'As soon as he'd seen the doctor, he headed back to Kansas.'

Steve's voice trailed off, and his head slumped forward again.

Cooney turned to Lassiter. 'Forget about them cows you were going for,' he said. 'I think Norton's telling the truth. Get nine men together as quick as you can, and ride out with them to that grove. I want Vickery. If he's there, kill him, and bury the body in the grove.

'If he ain't there, come back here. And make sure nobody in town hears about us holding Norton prisoner here.'

'What do we do with Norton?' asked Lassiter.

'We'll leave him strung up here for the time being,' said Cooney. 'Maybe we'll need to talk with him some more.'

SEVEN

At noon, on the day that Steve was taken prisoner at the Circle D, Lee was sitting against a boulder at the top of the wall of the ravine which he was using as a hiding-place. He was passing the time until he left to visit the store in Bledsoe that evening.

Facing the grove of trees that he had pointed out to Steve the previous day, he stiffened suddenly as he saw ten riders approaching the grove from the north. Splitting into three groups, the riders approached the grove from different directions, dismounted at its boundary, and moved inside on foot. Each man was holding a weapon in his hand.

It was clear to Lee that Steve's masquerade as Barclay had not succeeded. He knew that, only as a prisoner, would Steve hand out false information to Cooney which would cause the rancher to send men out to the grove.

Twenty minutes later, Lee saw the men leaving the grove. Two of them circled it at a distance, looking down at the ground. He guessed that they were looking for horse tracks. Lee himself had ridden over to take a look at the grove on the previous day, but he had been careful to leave no tracks which would help Cooney's men to find him in the ravine.

As he watched the Circle D hands, Lee knew that he must attempt to release his friend as soon as possible, if he was still alive. He saw that all ten Circle D hands were now riding away from the grove, heading north. He guessed that they were returning to the Circle D.

Lee rode into town well after nightfall. He thought it possible that Cooney might know he was in the area, and that he might have decided to have the store watched.

He left his horse on the edge of town. Then, keeping off the main street, and moving slowly and silently in the darkness, he came to a point from which he could observe the derelict shack from which Webster thought that Hoskins had kept a watch on the store recently.

He stood motionless for a few minutes, staring at the shack, but could see no sign of anyone there. He started moving towards the store, then stopped abruptly as a match flared close to a side wall of the shack, illuminating the face of a man who was standing there, lighting a cigarette.

The man looked like Hoskins, and Lee breathed a sigh of relief. The success of his plan to rescue Steve depended partly on the presence of Hoskins at the shack. He ran towards the rear of the store, making sure that Hoskins could see and hear him moving.

Reaching the door, he knocked on it, and Webster, who was expecting him, let him in. Hoskins saw the figure of a man pass through the doorway. As the door closed behind him, Lee spoke to the storekeeper.

'Hoskins is outside,' he said. 'I want to feed him some false information. He just saw somebody come in here, but he can't be sure that it's me. I reckon he'll want to find out. Can we sit talking in the living-room, with the window open and the curtains drawn back?'

'Sure,' said Webster. 'That's how we usually have them, on a hot evening like this.'

After a short conversation, the two men went into the living-room, the only room lighted at the time, where Lee greeted Abigail Webster. The storekeeper went out of the room with his wife, and returned a few minutes later, alone, closing the door behind him.

'When we hear a tap on the door,' said Webster, 'it'll mean that Abigail has spotted Hoskins listening outside the living-room window. She's watching from the bedroom.'

The two men sat down on armchairs close to the open window, and indulged in small talk until, five minutes after they had sat down, a tap came on the door.

'What're you planning to do next, Lee?' asked Webster, in a voice which, he felt sure, would carry to the man listening outside the window.

'I can't stay here any longer,' said Lee. 'I'm riding to Purdy tonight. I know that an old friend of mine is going to be there tomorrow. I aim to try and persuade him to help me to hand Cooney over to the law.'

Lee stood up. 'I'm leaving now,' he said. 'I'll get in touch when we get back.'

He left the room. Webster followed, closing the door behind him, and the two men waited outside the door until Abigail Webster came out of the bedroom and spoke to them.

'Hoskins took off a minute ago,' she said, 'and he was moving real fast.'

'He'll probably be riding out to the Circle D to see Cooney,' said Lee, 'and that's just where I'm going myself.'

He took his leave of the couple, and ran to his horse. He rode on to the street. Then, keeping in the shadows, he stopped and looked along the street towards the livery stable.

He did not have long to wait. In the light from the lamp hanging by the stable door he saw Hoskins lead his horse outside, mount it, and head in the direction of the Circle D. Lee, sure that Hoskins was on the way to see Cooney, followed him at a safe distance.

When, later on, he saw the outline of the Circle D buildings against the night sky, he rode off the trail and tied his horse to a bush. Then he ran towards the buildings, slowing down as he drew closer.

Carefully, he made his way towards the ranch house, and hid behind a big woodpile, not far from the door of the house.

Inside the house, Cooney, who had a little earlier received the news from Hoskins about the conversation between Lee and Webster, was giving orders to Lassiter. When the foreman left the house in a hurry, his departure was observed by Lee.

Fifteen minutes later, a group of fourteen

riders, led by Lassiter, rode up to the ranch house, and stopped in front of the rancher. They were followed by three men on foot. Cooney spoke to the ramrod. His words were clearly audible to Lee.

'You know what to do,' he said. 'Ride to Purdy, find Vickery, and kill him. And if he has his friend with him, kill him as well.'

'What about Norton?' asked Lassiter.

'We'll keep him alive for now,' Cooney replied. 'We'll leave him locked in the cabin. We'll get rid of him when you get back.'

The group of Circle D riders departed. Hoskins went for his horse and rode off towards Bledsoe.

Cooney spoke to the three men standing in front of him.

'Check on Norton just before you turn in, Brand,' he said, 'and you, Dixon, had better look in on him a couple of times during the night.'

Cooney turned and went inside. Brand and Dixon headed for the bunkhouse, and the third man, the cook, went into the cookshack. Lee, relieved to learn that Steve was still alive, followed the two men towards the bunkhouse. When they disappeared inside, he found a position from which he could keep the door of the bunkhouse under observation, and settled down to wait until Brand came out to check up on Steve.

When Cooney went back into the house, he spoke with two men, Hart and Bender, who had ridden in a few minutes after Hoskins arrived. They had been waiting to speak with Cooney. They said that they had heard that the rancher was looking for hands.

'That's right,' said Cooney. 'I'll take you on, provided a bit of law-breaking here and there don't bother you none.'

'We've always figured,' said Hart, 'that any law we don't like is just naturally there to be broken. When do we start?'

'Right now,' said Cooney. 'I'd like you to stay in the house while the foreman and the men with him are away. You can use the last two rooms along the passage at the top of the stairs.'

It was approaching midnight when Lee saw Brand come out of the bunkhouse carrying a lighted lamp, and walk over to a small cabin close by. He took a key from his pocket, unlocked a padlock on the door, and walked inside. After a few minutes, he reappeared, leaving the lighted lamp inside. He locked the padlock in place, then walked back to the bunkhouse, closing the door behind him. Shortly after this, the light in the bunkhouse was extinguished.

Lee waited for forty minutes, then moved silently to the door of the cabin, and felt the padlock. It was a stout one, and he knew that some effort would be needed to force it.

Looking round for something he could use for this purpose, he found, not far from the bunkhouse, a small covered area obviously used as a small blacksmith shop. He lit a match, looked round, and found a length of thick metal rod which he thought would serve his purpose.

He returned to the cabin door and used the leverage afforded by the rod to force the padlock, which gave way with a sound so slight that Lee thought it unlikely that it would have alerted the sleeping men in the bunkhouse.

He waited at the rear of the cabin for a few minutes. All appeared to be quiet in the bunkhouse. He moved back to the cabin door, opened it, and stepped inside. As he turned, after closing the door behind him, he was confronted by the spectacle of Steve, suspended against the wall of the cabin, his face puffed and bloody.

Lee cursed as he ran up to his friend. He lowered him to the floor, and untied his hands and feet.

'Looks like you took a real beating, Steve,' he said.

'Can't say I enjoyed it,' said Steve, 'and I sure am glad to see you. But it could have been worse. It's a good thing we thought up that plan about telling them that you were in the grove.'

'You fit to ride, Steve?' asked Lee.

'Just about, I reckon,' his friend replied. 'I

118

took a few punches in the ribs, but I don't think anything's busted. What do we do now?'

'We're leaving here,' said Lee, 'and we're taking Cooney with us. You've had a good look around here, Steve. Tell me where I'll find a couple of horses and saddles.'

'There's plenty of horses in the pasture,' Steve replied, 'and saddles and bridles in the shed near the gate.'

'You wait here,' said Lee, handing Steve his six-gun. 'From what I heard, nobody's going to check on you for a while yet. I'll get back as quick as I can. But before I go, let me tell you that fourteen armed riders have just left for Purdy on a wild-goose chase. They're expecting to find me there. Here on the ranch, there's one man in the cook-shack, two in the bunkhouse, and as far as I know, Cooney's alone in the house. Does that figure?'

Steve forced his aching head to do a little mental arithmetic.

'From what I've seen here,' he said, 'that

sounds about right.'

Lee left, and was back in twenty minutes. He called out softly, before entering the cabin. Inside, Steve, after checking up on his injuries, had been flexing his arms and legs.

'I've got three saddled horses waiting for us at the pasture fence,' said Lee. 'Now, before we go for Cooney, I reckon we should take care of the two hands and the cook. We don't want them interfering. I've got some rope outside. You OK, Steve?'

'Sure,' Steve replied. 'A bit sore around the middle, is all. Let's get started.'

They left the cabin, carrying the lamp with them, and approached the bunkhouse. It was still in darkness. Lee quietly opened the door and walked inside. Steve, carrying the lamp, followed him closely, and placed the lamp on a small table.

The two sleeping men jerked into shocked wakefulness as Lee roughly shook them, one after the other, then held his gun on them, while Steve removed their guns from the two gunbelts hanging close to them on the wall.

Then, while Steve held a gun on them, Lee trussed the couple in such a fashion that it would take them some considerable time to free themselves. Taking the six-guns belonging to Brand and Dixon, Lee and Steve left the bunkhouse.

Once outside, they threw one of the guns away, and Steve kept the other. They moved on to the cookshack, let themselves in through the unlocked door, and lit a lamp standing on a table inside. They entered the small built-on bedroom which had been provided for the cook, where they found him fast asleep. He received the same treatment as they had meted out to the men in the bunkhouse.

Inside the house, Cooney had been finding it difficult to sleep. He had been disturbed by the reappearance of Lee, and he was hoping that the mission of Lassiter, and the men with him, would be successful. After tossing and turning for some time, he got out of bed, and walked over to the bedroom window, which overlooked the cookshack.

He stood there looking out for a while, then decided to return to his bed. As he was turning away from the window, he saw, out of the corner of his eye, a movement outside. Turning back, he saw two shadowy figures pass through the cookshack door, to disappear inside. Moments later, a light, visible through chinks in the shutters, came on inside.

Cooney's sense of unease deepened. He could think of no reason for Brand and Dixon to visit the cookshack at this time of night. And it seemed to him that the two figures he had just seen were taller than the two ranch hands.

He dressed quickly, and went to rouse Hart and Bender. Having dressed, they came out of their rooms to join Cooney in the passage outside.

'You can start earning your money right now,' he told them. 'I was looking out of my bedroom window a few minutes ago, and I saw two men go into the cookshack. I'm pretty sure they ain't Circle D hands, and there's a chance it could be Vickery and some friend of his. It might even be Vickery and Norton. They could be coming in here next.'

He handed a loaded shotgun to Hart. 'You two go downstairs,' he said, 'and unbolt the door to the outside, but leave it closed. I'm staying up here to watch the cookshack. If I see the two men coming towards the house, I'll call you. As soon as they've opened the door and are stepping inside, let them have a couple of loads of buckshot. And let me know as soon as you've finished them off.'

As Cooney hurried back to his bedroom window, Bender and Hart went downstairs to the living-room. Bender felt his way over to the door leading to the outside, and slid the bolt back. Then he and Hart crouched behind a large armchair that was facing the door. Hart was holding the shotgun, while Bender had a revolver in his hand.

Upstairs, Cooney was keeping watch on the cookshack. It was not long before he saw the light go out inside, and the same two shadowy figures leave the cookshack, and move towards the door of the house. As they came up close to the front wall of the house, they passed out of Cooney's view.

The rancher hurried to the foot of the stairs, to tell Hart and Bender that two men were approaching the door. Then he went back upstairs, and stood at the top, listening.

Lee and Steve moved silently up to the door, and stood against it, listening. Suddenly, Lee felt a strong premonition of danger. He gently turned the door handle and pushed the edge of the door inwards for a couple of inches. Then he drew Steve to the wall at the side of the door.

'I may be wrong, Steve,' he whispered, 'but something tells me that all hell's going to bust loose the minute we walk through that door. Wait here.'

He went to the woodpile behind which he had hidden earlier, and picked up a metal rake, with a long wooden handle, which he had seen standing against the pile. From the top of the pile, he removed two pieces of waterproof sheet.

He cut two short slits near one end of each of the two sheets, then pushed the rake handle through the four slits, so that the sheets were hanging from the end of the handle adjacent to the rake. Then he returned to Steve.

With his friend close by him, Lee stood against the wall at one side of the door. Holding the handle, he pressed the end of the rake hard against the door, and pushed it wide open. Then he held the handle so that the two sheets were suspended in the wide doorway.

Hart and Bender heard the squeak of the opening door, and in the darkness, they got the vague impression of two figures standing in the doorway. Hart fired off both barrels of his shotgun, and Bender fired two shots from his six-gun.

Lee jerked the rake away from the door, and threw it down on the ground. At the same time, both he and Steve gave a loud yell of simulated pain, tailing off into silence.

Holding their six-guns, Hart and Bender both ran to the door and bent down to look at the two pieces of sheeting lying crumpled on the ground outside. At the same instant, both men realized that they were not looking at the bodies of two men riddled with buckshot. Desperately, they straightened up and looked around.

A few paces away, they saw the dim shapes of Lee and Steve, standing side by side, and turned to bring their guns to bear on them. But before they had completed the move, there was a twin blast from the six-shooters in the hands of Lee and Steve, and Hart and Bender, both shot in the chest, staggered back, and fell to the ground.

Lee and Steve ran up to pick up the guns of the two men, which had fallen to the ground. Hart was lying motionless. Bender slowly raised himself up on one elbow, then slumped down again, and lay still.

Lee checked the two men.

'They're both dead,' he said, 'and I reckon they had it coming. Imagine what that shotgun blast would have done to the two of us if we'd been standing in the doorway.'

Suddenly, Lee realized that neither of the two men lying on the ground was of similar build to Cooney. He flattened himself against the wall of the house, taking Steve with him.

'Cooney must be inside,' he whispered. 'I figure those two were guarding him.'

He looked up at the three bedroom windows above him.

'Are those three windows the only ones on the upper floor?' he asked Steve.

'That's right,' Steve replied.

'I'm going in after Cooney,' said Lee. 'You stay here in case he tries to make a run for it through one of those bedroom windows. Where are the stairs located inside?'

'In the back left-hand corner of the living-room,' Steve replied. 'You take care in there.' He moved just around the corner, to stand against the side wall of the house, while Lee crawled through the doorway, then stood against the wall to the left of it.

Cooney was still upstairs. He heard the sounds of shotgun and pistol fire, followed by a brief pause, then more pistol fire. He waited for Hart or Bender to call up the stairs to let him know that the two intruders had been blasted into oblivion. But he waited in vain.

Realizing that something was sadly amiss, he went into his bedroom, eased the window open, and poked his head through the aperture. He saw, just outside the front door, what appeared to be two motionless bodies lying on the ground. He had to assume that they were Hart and Bender. There was no sign of the two men he had seen approaching the door earlier. He guessed that they were in the house.

He climbed out of the window, hung down, with his hands gripping the sill, then dropped to the ground and fell sideways. As he was rising to his feet, Steve came up behind him. He picked the rancher's six-gun from its holster, threw it aside, and held the muzzle of his own revolver against the side of Cooney's head. Then he called to Lee, who came running out of the house to join them.

Lee stood in front of the rancher.

'You're finished Cooney,' he said. 'We're taking you to Amarillo for trial. There's a lady there who's going to tell the judge just what happened to my parents. I reckon that my testimony and hers'll send you straight to the gallows.'

While Steve held a gun on Cooney, Lee went into the bunkhouse and spoke to the two bound men inside.

'Cooney's been captured,' he told them. 'We're taking him in for trial for murder and other things. When Lassiter and the others get back, tell them that, and say that the law's likely to start looking for them when it hears what Cooney's been up to here in the valley.'

Lee returned to the house, then he and Steve escorted Cooney to the three saddled horses, and they rode towards town.

Leaving the other two on the outskirts, Lee rode on to the store, roused Webster, and told him that they had captured Cooney, and were taking him to Amarillo.

They reached Amarillo, without incident, two days later, and handed their prisoner over to US Marshal Bantry, who was stationed there. Lee told Bantry about Cooney's criminal activities in the Bledsoe area, and he was tried two weeks later, with Lee, Steve and Kate, who had been located at one of the saloons in town, as witnesses.

Cooney was sentenced to death by hanging, and the sentence was duly carried out on the following day. After the hanging, Lee and Steve went to Marshal Bantry's office.

'I figure,' said the marshal, 'that you're aiming to go after that man Brady, who killed your mother.'

'That's right,' said Lee. 'I came to ask you if you know anything about Brady that might help me to find him.'

'He's an outlaw,' said Bantry, 'and his gun

is for hire. He's wanted in Kansas, Texas and Indian Territory. He usually works alone, but sometimes he joins up with a gang led by an outlaw called Jed Barrow. Barrow's the worst kind of outlaw, liable to kill anybody who gets in his way.

'But I've got no idea where he's likely to be just now. Sorry I can't help. But if you do happen to meet up with him in the Panhandle, let me know, and I'll ask the ranger captain here to send some men out to pick him up.'

Lee and Steve left the marshal's office, and went along to the saloon where Kate was working. They both asked for a beer, and sat down at a table. Kate saw them, and came over.

'You boys staying on in Amarillo for a while?' she asked.

'No,' replied Lee, 'I'm aiming to take off after Brady. Trouble is, I ain't got the faintest notion of where to start.'

Kate puckered her brow, and was silent for a few moments. Then she spoke.

'I've just remembered something,' she said. 'Maybe it'll help. When I was out on the veranda of the saloon in Bledsoe, listening to Cooney and Brady talking in one of the rooms, I heard Brady say something about a job in Drury, but I didn't hear any details. I just happen to remember the name, because that's what an uncle of mine is called.'

'Drury,' said Lee. 'Can't say I've heard of it. How about you, Steve?'

'Same here,' Steve replied.

'Wherever it is,' said Lee, 'I'm going to ride there. If I do that, maybe I can get on Brady's trail.'

Lee thanked Kate, then walked with Steve to the telegraph office along the street. He asked the operator if he knew of a place called Drury.

'I've heard the name,' said the operator, 'but I just can't remember where it's located.'

He pulled a tattered bundle of papers from a shelf in front of him, and looked through them till he found what he wanted.

'According to this,' he said, 'there's a town called Drury in Indian Territory, not far south-west of Caldwell, over the border in Kansas.'

They thanked the operator and went to see Marshal Bantry. Lee told him what Kate had said.

'I know of Drury,' the marshal said, 'because I have a cousin running the livery stable there. His name's Barton, Hank Barton. Talk with him when you get there. Maybe he can help you.'

Lee thanked the marshal. He and Steve left the office and stood on the boardwalk outside.

'Well, Steve,' said Lee to his friend, 'I guess here's where we part company. I sure owe you for the way you've helped me to get the better of Cooney.'

'You ain't going to get rid of me that easy,' said Steve. 'I'm going with you. I ain't got nothing better to do, and I reckon you're going to need some help.'

'I don't know how long it'll take,' said Lee, 'and maybe you'll end up dead. Brady's a dangerous man, and he has some dangerous friends.'

'I reckon we can get the better of them if we team up together,' said Steve. 'Now stop arguing, and tell me when you're figuring to leave.'

'In the morning,' Lee replied. 'And thanks, Steve. I'll sure be glad of your company.'

EIGHT

Lee and Steve rode out of Amarillo the following morning, heading east, and four days later, as they breasted a rise, they spotted Drury about a mile ahead. As they approached the small town, two riders left it, and galloped up to meet them.

The riders came to a halt in front of Lee and Steve. Each of them was carrying a six-gun. One of them was short, the other of average height. Both were bearded. Two hardbitten characters, thought Lee, who certainly didn't have the look of townsmen.

The short man spoke.

'This is as far as you go,' he said. 'The town's closed. We've got the cholera in Drury. Twenty people dead already. The hotel's closed, and the saloon and livery stable as well.'

'That's bad news,' said Lee. 'We were planning on staying in Drury for the night. You say nobody's allowed in town?'

'That's right,' said the short man. 'It's for your own good.'

'We'll be riding on, then,' said Lee. 'We'll camp out on the trail.'

Lee and Steve headed off in a direction which would bypass Drury. Behind them, the two riders watched them for a while, then rode back into town.

'What d'you make of that?' Lee asked his friend.

'The man was lying,' said Steve. 'I've met up with enough criminals in my time to get the feeling that those two are up to no good.'

'I reckon you're right,' said Lee, 'and I'm mighty curious about why they don't want us to ride into town. Let's make camp out of sight of town, then we'll sneak in after dark, and see what we can find out. We'll call on Marshal Bantry's cousin.'

They camped in a hollow off the trail, on

the east side of Drury. They waited there till well after nightfall, then rode towards Drury, keeping well away from the main trails leading into town. Leaving their horses tethered on the outskirts of town, they made their way towards the centre of town, keeping off the main street.

When they judged that they were not far from the centre of town they slipped along an alley between two buildings, and looked out on to the main street, which was deserted at the time. On the opposite side of the street they could see the swing-doors of a saloon, with lights showing inside. The windows of the saloon were open, and they could hear the sound of voices inside.

'It don't look like a closed saloon to me,' said Steve. Looking at one of the two buildings adjacent to the saloon, they could just make out the words: LIVERY STABLE HANK BARTON PROP. painted on the front of it. First checking that the street was still deserted, they ran across it, passed through an alley, and approached the livery stable from the rear. A light was showing in the house built on to the back of the stable. Lee knocked on the door.

It was opened by the liveryman Hank Barton, who stared at the two strangers standing outside.

'We'd appreciate a few words with you, Mr Barton,' said Lee. 'Your cousin, Marshal Bantry, in Amarillo, reckoned you might be able to help us.'

Barton stepped back. 'Come on in,' he said, urgently, and quickly closed the door behind them.

'Did anybody see you come here?' he asked.

'Not that we know of,' Lee replied, and introduced himself and Steve to the liveryman, who took them into the living-room, where they all sat down.

'You got a cholera epidemic in town?' asked Lee.

Surprised at the question, Barton shook his head.

'Who told you that?' he asked. 'We had

some cases two years ago, but nothing since.'

'Earlier today,' said Lee, 'we were riding towards town, when two men stopped us. They said the town was closed because of a cholera epidemic.'

'They would be Barrow's men,' said the livery-man.

Lee exchanged glances with Steve, as Barton went on to tell them how the Barrow gang, numbering six outlaws in all, had ridden into town the previous evening. Before anybody realized what was happening, they had rounded up, at gunpoint, the wives of the storekeeper and the blacksmith, and their children of whom there were three.

The women and children had been taken to the schoolhouse, where they were being guarded by two members of the gang. Barrow had then told the townspeople that he and his men were taking the town over for a couple of days, and if any of them gave him any trouble, such as sending for help from outside, the women and children in the schoolhouse would suffer.

Barton went on to say that Barrow had taken over one of the rooms at the hotel, with an adjoining room being used by two other members of the gang. These two changed over, about every four hours, with the two guards in the schoolhouse.

'Did Barrow give his reason for coming here?' asked Lee.

'No,' replied Barton, 'but we've been thinking about that. We reckon that maybe he aims to rob the stagecoach. It's due in town tomorrow, around eleven in the morning.

'Loomey, the man who runs the stage office here don't know for sure whether there's a valuable shipment on board, but he reckons there could be. And he figures that Barrow might think it's safer to do the unexpected, and steal the shipment here in town.'

'You're sure it's Barrow and his gang?' asked Lee.

'It's Barrow all right,' Barton replied. 'The

blacksmith recognized him. He was on a visit to Caldwell about five months ago. He happened to see the gang when they were robbing a bank there. The blacksmith was inside the bank when it happened, and he got a good look at Barrow.'

Lee explained to the liveryman that he was trying to find a man called Brady, who had murdered his mother on the Box V ranch in the Texas Panhandle. He gave Barton a description of the killer which he himself had received from Kate.

'Sometimes Brady worked with Barrow,' said Lee. 'Was he with the Barrow gang when they rode into town?'

'He was,' Barton replied. 'I saw the scar over his eye, and I happened to overhear one of the others call him Brady. But he ain't here now. He rode out of town early this morning. I don't know where he was headed. But I did overhear something else that might help.

'Just after he picked up his horse, I overheard him talking to Barrow outside the stable. He told Barrow that he'd see them at the hideout. He said he'd go there as soon as he'd taken care of Leary. Then he rode off.'

'Does the name Leary mean anything to you?' asked Lee.

'No, it don't,' Barton replied, 'nor to any of the townsfolk here.'

Lee considered the situation. If he and Steve could help the townsfolk to overcome the Barton gang, maybe one of the outlaws could be persuaded to reveal the whereabouts of the person called Leary.

He had a few words with Steve while Barton was attending to a brief chore in the stable. When the liveryman had finished, Lee spoke to him.

'My friend and I,' he said, 'have both been deputy sheriffs in Kansas. We'd like to help you and your friends to capture the Barrow gang before they do what they came here for. D'you think we can count on any help from the men living here in town?'

'Not while the women and children are being held in the schoolhouse,' said Barton.

'If it weren't for that, I can think of two men as well as myself who're handy with a gun, and who'd be willing to help.'

'Good,' said Lee. 'Then it's clear that the first thing we have to do is free the prisoners in the schoolhouse. Is there any way we can get in there without the guards knowing it, so's we can surprise them?'

'Not that I knows of,' Barton replied. 'There's only one door leading in from the outside, and that faces on to the street. There are three windows in the schoolhouse, but I can't see any of them being opened from outside without the guards being alerted.

'Until a few years ago, the schoolhouse and the doctor's house next to it were one building which was used as a store. Then the owner died, and a dividing wall was built inside, so that the doctor and the school-house could both be accommodated.

'Most of the work was done by Ken Morse, who lives just along the street. Would you like a word with him? He's a good friend of mine.'

'A good idea,' said Lee. 'Maybe he can help us.'

Barton returned with Morse ten minutes later, and introduced him to Lee and Steve.

'I've told him what you want to do,' he said, 'and he reckons there might be a way.'

'There's a roof space running along the whole building,' said Morse, 'and the floor's boarded over. There's a trapdoor into this space through the ceiling of a small store-room in the back corner of the schoolhouse.

'When I was working on dividing the building, the doctor asked me to build a trapdoor in the ceiling of his bedroom, which gave access to the roof space, and I did this for him.'

'So there's a good chance of us being able to get into the schoolhouse storeroom without the guards knowing?' asked Lee.'

'I reckon so,' Morse replied. 'The school trapdoor can be opened from above.'

'I reckon,' said Lee, 'that we should go ahead and free the prisoners. From what I've heard of Barrow, he's a dangerous killer.

What if things go wrong during his operation, and he decides to take it out on the women and children?'

'I think you're right,' said Barton, 'but it's up to Brent and Haley. They're the ones whose families are in there. I'll go and ask them. They happen to be the two men I told you about who'd probably be willing to help you if the prisoners hadn't been taken.'

'Could you bring them back here?' asked Lee. 'If they agree about freeing the prisoners, maybe we can work out a plan together.'

'I'll do that,' said Barton, 'but I'll have to make sure we ain't spotted by any of the gang.'

He returned fifteen minutes later, with Brent, the blacksmith, and Haley, the store-keeper. After a short discussion, the two men agreed that an attempt should be made to free the prisoners. Some time was then spent on deciding a plan of action for an operation which must be carried out before daybreak.

After Barton had slipped out and returned

with the confirmation that Doc Mallory, and Hix, the owner of the hotel, were willing to co-operate, the six men settled down to wait.

Leaving the others, Barton sat in the dark, in an adjoining bedroom, looking through the window towards the door of the school-house along the street. Light was showing through the chinks in the shutters covering the windows.

NINE

Just before midnight, Barton rejoined the others.

'The guards have just changed over,' he told them, 'and the two who were in the schoolhouse have gone into the hotel.'

'We'll give them all an hour to settle down,' said Lee, 'then we'll make a start.'

At half an hour past midnight, Barton slipped over to the hotel to see Hix, the owner. He was back in ten minutes, to report that Barrow and the other two outlaws had all gone to their rooms half an hour earlier.

Lee and Steve, accompanied by Brent and Haley, made their way to a side entrance to the doctor's house. The door was not locked. Silently, they slipped inside, and closed the door behind them.

Doc Mallory appeared, holding a lighted

147

oil-lamp in his hand. He was a slim, bearded man, in his early sixties. He beckoned to them to follow him into his bedroom. He put the lamp down on a table.

'There it is,' he said, pointing towards the trapdoor in the ceiling, with a stepladder standing underneath it. 'You can use a lamp to see your way when you get up there. I'll light this other lamp on the table here.'

Lee climbed up the stepladder, pushed the trapdoor upwards, twisted it, then lowered it down and handed it to Steve. The doctor handed him one of the lamps, which Lee placed inside the loft, then climbed up after it. He was followed by Steve, Brent and Haley. The four men stood near the trapdoor opening.

'You two stay here till we call you,' whispered Lee to the two townsmen. 'And the less noise we all make, the better.'

Taking the lamp, and with Steve close behind him, carrying a coil of rope, Lee moved carefully along the floor of the loft until he reached the trapdoor in the ceiling of the schoolhouse storeroom.

With infinite care, he lifted the trapdoor slightly, to check that there was no light inside the storeroom underneath. He removed the trapdoor, and carefully laid it aside. Then, with the aid of the lamp, he checked that the floor underneath the trapdoor was clear.

Leaving the lamp in the loft, Lee took off his boots, then lowered himself through the aperture and dropped to the floor of the storeroom. A moment later Steve, also bootless, was standing beside him.

Looking towards the door leading to the schoolroom, they could see a chink of light at the bottom. They moved up to the door. Lee carefully lifted the latch and eased the door open a fraction, praying that the hinges would not squeak. His prayer was answered.

Looking through the narrow gap into the schoolroom, he could see Walker, one of the two guards, sitting on a chair near to the door leading to the street. His partner, Melville, apparently asleep, was lying on the floor, covered by a blanket. Only his head and shoulders were visible.

Lee could not see the women and children. They must, he thought, be along the rear wall of the schoolroom, which was out of his view.

He whispered to Steve, who picked up a broom which was standing against the wall and moved to a position underneath the trapdoor. He poked the broom up through the opening as far as he could reach, then withdrew it. He repeated this twice.

In the loft, Brent saw the signal, and whispered to the doctor down below. Mallory picked up the lighted lamp, and took it into a room which had a window looking out on to the street. He placed the lamp in front of the window, left it there for a minute, then took it back to the bedroom.

The watching Barton saw the signal, and left the stable, carrying a small bag of stones. Moving in the shadows close to the buildings, he reached a point a little over twenty yards from the schoolhouse. From where he was standing, he had a clear view of the front of the building.

He took a stone from the bag, and threw it towards the door of the schoolhouse. It hit the top of the door, and fell on to the step down below.

Inside the schoolroom, Walker stiffened on his seat, and looked towards the door. Moments later, a second and larger stone, propelled by Barton, hit the door.

Walker stood up, lifted his revolver from its holster, and ran over to prod his sleeping partner in the ribs with his boot.

'Get up,' he said. 'There's somebody outside.'

Melville threw off the blanket, and as he rose to his feet, picking his six-gun off the floor, a third stone hit the door. The two guards, in full view of Lee, stood side by side, their eyes glued to the door, listening intently for any further sounds outside.

Lee, closely followed by Steve, pushed the door of the storeroom open and stepped into the schoolroom. They saw the two women seated against the wall, with their children lying nearby. Both women were awake, and they stared, open-mouthed, as Lee and Steve ran quickly across the room in stockinged feet, and came up behind the two outlaws.

At the last moment, Walker sensed that there was someone behind him, and he started to swing round. But he was too late. He had only half-completed the turn when the barrel of Lee's six-gun struck him on the side of the head.

Simultaneously, Melville was expertly pistol-whipped from behind by Steve. The outlaws, both stunned, slumped to the floor, and were immediately gagged, and securely bound by their captors.

Steve went back into the storeroom and called to Brent and Haley, who dropped from the loft to join their families.

'You two stay here with your wives and children,' said Lee, 'and keep an eye on these two outlaws. We'll let you know when we've taken care of the others.'

Lee and Steve left the schoolhouse. After telling the doctor what had happened they went to the stable, where Barton and Morse were waiting. They told them that the two outlaws in the schoolhouse had been taken prisoner.

'Now for the other three,' said Lee. 'Do we know which rooms they're in at the hotel?'

'Sure,' said Barton. 'Hix told me earlier. Barrow's in room four, and the other two are in room three.'

The four men left the stable, and walked over to the hotel, where Hix was waiting to let them in. He pointed to a large metal drum standing in the lobby. It was a container, normally used for storing water. It had three metal feet and two carrying-handles.

'I got this ready, like you asked,' he said. 'There's some rags in there, and plenty of other stuff that'll give us what we want. And there's nobody upstairs but the three outlaws.'

'Good,' said Lee. 'I figured this was the

best way of making sure that none of us gets hurt.'

He fastened a bandanna around his face, so that his mouth and nose were well covered. Steve did the same, then the two of them, moving as quietly as possible, carried the drum upstairs and stood it at the beginning of the passage that led to the bedroom doors. Rooms three and four were side by side, half-way along the passage.

According to Hix, the doors of the rooms were stout, and the locks strong, so that bursting in without alerting the occupants would not be an easy task. Hix had also told them that the window in each of the rooms was jammed tight.

Lee lit a match, and dropped it into the small hole which had been left in the centre of the pile of material in the drum. Some dry shavings at the bottom of the drum caught fire and it was not long before thick smoke was billowing out. Lee and Steve carried the drum to the end of the passage, then retreated to the stairs, where they waited while the smoke filtered into the rooms through the gaps between the doors and the frames.

Barrow was the first to be awakened by the presence of smoke in his room. Coughing, he left the bed, ran over to the door, and unlocked it. As he opened it, he was enveloped in a cloud of thick smoke which sent him into a paroxysm of coughing. He staggered along the passage to the top of the stairs, stumbled down them, still coughing uncontrollably, and collapsed at the feet of Lee and Steve, waiting for him at the bottom.

He was closely followed by his two men, Floyd and Carr, who had been awakened by the noise outside their room, and who were in a similar condition to Barrow. The three outlaws, clad only in their long johns, were in no condition for a fight, and Barton held a gun on them while Lee and Steve, noses and mouths covered, ran up to the smoking drum, slapped on it the lid which belonged to it, and carried it downstairs and out into the street.

Then they went back into the hotel, where the three outlaws were lying on the floor, still coughing. Helped by the others, they dragged Barrow and his men out on to the boardwalk, and tied their hands behind them.

'We might as well stay out here till the smoke clears a bit,' said Lee. 'Is there somewhere we can hold Barrow and his men prisoner till the law gets here?'

'We might as well keep them all in the schoolhouse,' Barton replied. 'It ain't going to be used for the next two weeks. And I'm sure I can find plenty of men who'll be willing to take a turn guarding them. But we'd be grateful if you and your friend would stay around and organize the guarding of the prisoners till the law turns up.'

'Sure,' said Lee. 'We'll do that.'

'Good,' said Barton. 'I'm going to see the telegraph operator first thing in the morning to get him to send a message to the US marshal at Fort Smith, asking him to send some deputies as soon as he can, to pick up the prisoners. They sure will be pleased to get their hands on the Barrow gang.'

'As soon as the deputies turn up,' said Lee, 'Steve and me will be going after the man Brady, who murdered my mother. I reckon that Barrow and his men knew where Brady was going when he left here. But it ain't likely they're going to tell us.'

He paused, as a thought suddenly struck him. Then he continued.

'I just had an idea,' he said. 'I'd like Mr Morse to do something for me in the schoolhouse that I don't want the prisoners to see. We'll go there now, and Steve'll bring the two prisoners back here for a while. What Mr Morse has to do won't take long. When he's finished, we'll put all the prisoners in the schoolhouse.'

Lee and Steve, accompanied by Morse, went to the schoolhouse, and told Brent and Haley that it was now safe to take their wives and children home. After they had left, Steve escorted the two prisoners to the hotel.

Half an hour later, Lee and Morse

returned to the hotel, and all the prisoners were escorted to the schoolhouse, and seated with their backs to the side wall, close to the storeroom. They were all now fully dressed, and their hands and feet were bound.

Lee and Steve volunteered to guard the prisoners for the next four hours, and Barton offered to arrange for relief guards at four-hour intervals thereafter. The two guards were to sit on chairs, facing the prisoners, and each guard was to carry a loaded shotgun.

Around two o'clock the following morning, after a few hours' sleep, Lee walked to the doctor's house, climbed into the loft and, using a ladder which had been placed under the trapdoor, descended into the schoolhouse storeroom. The door of the room, which was visible to the prisoners, was closed.

Lee moved silently to a corner of the storeroom, where a circular hole, about six inches in diameter, had been cut, at head height, in the partition wall between the storeroom and the schoolroom. The hole was concealed by the blackboard fixed to the wall in the schoolroom.

The hole had been cut by Morse during the earlier visit by him and Lee to the empty schoolhouse. At the same time, Morse had refixed the blackboard so that it stood out slightly from the surface to which it was fixed. The blackboard was close to the prisoners.

The two guards in the schoolroom stood up as the door from the street opened, and Barton called to them to go outside. Before doing this, they inspected the ropes which were binding the prisoners.

Inside the schoolroom, the prisoners remained silent until the guards had disappeared outside. Lee, with his ear against the hole in the partition, listened to the ensuing conversation.

'How do we get out of this fix, Jed?' asked one voice, with a hint of panic in it. 'It ain't going to be long before them deputies turn up.'

Barrow's harsh, deep voice replied:

'It ain't going to be easy,' he said. 'They're watching us too close.'

The prisoners then spent some time discussing possible ways of outwitting the guards, and Lee was beginning to lose hope that he would hear anything that would help him in his search for Brady.

Then he heard one of the men ask Barrow whether there was any chance of Brady getting help to them.

'If he found Leary in Northam,' said Barrow, 'and I'm pretty sure he would, then as soon as he'd killed him like I asked him to, he was going to visit his cousin Cliff Jordan, before meeting up with us. Likely we'll be well on the way to Fort Smith before Brady hears about what's happened here.'

Lee stayed another fifteen minutes, listening to the conversation, but there was no further mention of Brady. He left by way of the loft and the doctor's house, and signalled to the guards to return to the schoolhouse.

As he was walking towards the livery stable

the stagecoach rolled past him and stopped outside the stage office. A shotgun rider was sitting on the box beside the driver. The passengers climbed down, and went inside the hotel for a meal.

Loomey, the agent, spoke with the driver, then came over to Barton, standing with Lee and Steve outside the stable.

'There's a big gold shipment on board,' he said. 'Barrow must have got wind of it somehow.'

Twice more, during the day, the guards left the schoolhouse while Lee eavesdropped in the storeroom, but he heard nothing further which would help him find Brady. It was clear that the prisoners were getting more and more concerned about their fate.

He made three similar visits to the storeroom over the next two days, with similar results. At mid-morning on the following day, two deputies arrived with a jail wagon, and the prisoners were handed over.

Lee had a word with Sweeney, the elder of

the two deputies. He told him of his pursuit of Brady, and what he had heard while eavesdropping in the schoolhouse.

'I've seen Wanted notices on Brady and Leary,' said Sweeney. 'They've both worked with Barrow at one time or another. I'm wondering why Barrow wanted Leary killed. You know where Northam is, do you?'

'I know it's east of here,' said Lee, 'and not far from the Kansas border.'

'That's right,' said Sweeney, 'it's about sixty-five miles east of here, and twelve miles south of the border. As for Brady's cousin Cliff Jordan, I ain't heard of him before.'

'What does this Leary look like?' asked Lee.

'As far as I can remember,' Sweeney replied, 'he was a short man, on the skinny side, with red hair.'

'Thanks,' said Lee. 'We'll ride on to Northam, and try to pick up Brady's trail.'

'There's a sheriff in Caldwell,' said Sweeney, 'who might know something about

Brady's cousin. His name's Pearce. He's been a lawman for a long time.'

'I've heard of him,' said Lee. 'Maybe we'll call on him.'

TEN

Lee and Steve left Drury just after noon, and camped out on the trail overnight. They reached Northam during the afternoon of the following day. Reckoning that the barkeep was likely to have an intimate knowledge of all the recent happenings in town, they went into the saloon.

They were the only customers. They ordered beers, and engaged the barkeep in conversation. It was not long before they learnt of a killing which had taken place two days earlier.

The victim, who had been knifed in the back, was a man who called himself Ross. He had arrived in town about a month ago, and had rented a shack on the edge of town. He was pretty closemouthed, and nobody knew anything about him. From some

165

papers found in the shack, it looked like his real name was Leary. Nobody knew who the killer was.

'Around the time of the murder,' said Lee, 'was there a tall, slim stranger around, with a scar over his eye?'

'There was,' replied the barkeep. 'He was in here a couple of times. He left the same day the body was found, heading west. You reckon he had something to do with the killing?'

'We know he did,' said Lee. 'He's an outlaw called Brady. We're on his trail.'

'I'm wondering,' said Steve, as they left the saloon, 'what Leary did to Barrow that made Barrow have him killed.'

'I've been wondering the same thing myself,' said Lee. 'Probably he double-crossed Barrow in some way. Maybe we'll never know exactly what happened. Let's head for Caldwell in the morning.'

They reached Caldwell late the next day, and on the following morning, when they had finished breakfast, they went to the office of Sheriff Pearce. A rangy man in his sixties, with a drooping moustache, he was seated behind his desk.

Lee introduced himself and Steve, and told Pearce about their search for Brady, and the reason for it. He also told him about the downfall of the Barrow gang, and the death of Leary.

'That's good news about Barrow and his gang,' said the sheriff. 'I've spent a lot of time chasing them in the past, but never managed to catch up with them.'

'D'you know Brady and his cousin Jordan?' asked Lee.

'Brady's an outlaw,' Pearce replied. 'I've heard a lot about him, but I never met him. Jordan I have met. He ran a cattle ranch west of here until two years ago. I was pretty sure he was rustling cattle, but I never managed to get the proof.

'I reckon he got tired of us nosing around, because he moved to the Texas Panhandle, and started ranching there.'

'That's interesting,' said Lee, 'because

we're pretty certain that when Brady left Northam, he was on his way to visit Jordan. D'you know exactly where Jordan's ranch is located?'

'I don't,' the sheriff replied, 'but I know who does. Go and see Hal Bailey. He runs three big freight wagons, and he moved some furniture and ranch machinery for Jordan. His office is on the south side of town.'

They thanked Pearce and went to see Bailey, who was in his office. He told them that Jordan's Double J Ranch was located about ten miles south of Purdy, the place where Lee and Steve had encountered Morg Barclay and Tracy not so long ago.

'Quite a coincidence,' commented Steve, as they were walking away from Bailey's office. 'We ride there, do we?'

'We sure do,' Lee replied. 'I've a strong hunch that we'll find Brady there.'

'A chance to see Miriam again then?' said Steve, well aware that his friend and the girl had been strongly attracted to one another.

'That's right,' said Lee. 'I'm looking forward to it. Might as well leave now.'

At the time that Lee and Steve were about to leave Caldwell, Brady was at the Double J ranch in the Texas Panhandle, run by his cousin, Cliff Jordan. Brady, who was not known in Purdy, had just returned from a visit there.

While he was in the saloon, a drummer who was peddling liquor came in with some items of news which grabbed the attention of the barkeep and the customers, particularly Brady. According to the drummer, he had been travelling westward through Indian Territory, selling his wares, when he called in at a place called Northam, just after a man called Brady had killed another man called Leary, before disappearing.

But the big, sensational news brought by the drummer had come from Drury, where the Barrow gang had been planning to rob the stage. The plan had been thwarted by two strangers called Vickery and Norton, and the gang, including the leader, had been captured, and taken to Fort Smith.

The drummer had said that it turned out that Vickery and Norton had been trailing Brady, who had murdered Vickery's mother. And when they had left Drury, they were aiming to find the ranch belonging to some relative of Brady's, where Brady might be hiding.

Considerably shaken by the news, Brady had returned to the Double J, where he told Jordan what he had heard.

'D'you reckon that Vickery's been able to find out where the Double J is located?' asked Brady.

'Probably,' replied Jordan. 'Vickery and his partner could be on their way here right now.'

'We've got to watch out for them,' said Brady. 'Once we know where they are, I'll finish them off. I don't like being trailed. Will you ask the ramrod to tell all the hands to be on the look-out for Vickery and Norton.'

Jordan nodded. 'I'm paying a man called Miller, in Purdy, to let me know about anything interesting going on there,' he said. 'He helps out in the saloon. I'll make sure he watches out for Vickery and his friend, and lets us know right away if he turns up.'

'About that job you want me to do for you,' said Brady. 'We'd better put it off till I've dealt with those two.'

'All right,' agreed Jordan. 'I'll go and see the ramrod now. I'll tell him to station one man in Drury, to co-operate with Miller, and with orders to report back here pronto if Vickery and his partner show up. The others'll keep their eyes open for any strangers crossing our range.'

During the next three days there were no sightings of Lee and Steve by Jordan's hands, but on the afternoon of the fourth day a hand called Kelly came riding in fast, and ran into the ranch house.

He told Jordan and Brady that he'd been looking for strays to the east of the range. While taking a rest in the shade of some trees he'd seen two men riding by, close enough for him to recognize them as Vickery and Norton.

'I saw them both in Purdy,' he said, 'the time they shot dead a man who was trying to kill Norton. When I saw them today they were heading west, maybe for Purdy. I thought about following them, but there weren't no cover to speak of, and I reckon they'd have spotted me. So I came to tell you.'

'You done right,' said Jordan. 'If they ride into Purdy, our man there'll let us know.'

'If they don't,' said Kelly, 'I've got an idea where they might've been heading. I was in Purdy again soon after that shooting I mentioned. It seems that Vickery was found, out on the range, with a bullet in him, by the daughter of Pete Randle, who runs the Crazy R.

'The story was that Vickery and the girl had taken a shine to one another, and when he'd taken care of some unfinished business, Vickery was going to come back to her.'

'That's very interesting,' said Brady.

When by noon on the following day no report had been received of the arrival of Lee and Steve in Purdy, Jordan and Brady thought it probable that they had made contact with the Randles, and they started thinking up a plan designed to eliminate them.

Towards the end of their long ride to the Texas Panhandle, Lee and Steve had decided to hide out somewhere in the Purdy area until they had discovered whether Brady was on the Double J with Jordan. They decided to ride straight to the Crazy R, to see if the Randles could give them any useful information.

They rode up to the ranch house just after dark, and Miriam answered the knock on the door. Her face lit up with pleasure and relief as she saw Lee, and she led them into the living-room, where her parents, and Wes Tucker, the foreman, were seated. When the greetings were over, Lee explained that he and Steve suspected that Brady, the murderer of his mother, was staying at the Double J. If he was, they intended to capture him, and hand him over to the law.

'What does this Brady look like?' asked Wes Tucker.

Lee described Brady, mentioning the scar above his eye.

'Well, I'm danged,' said Tucker. 'I'm near certain I was standing next to him at the saloon bar in Purdy a few days ago. There was a drummer in there, telling how you two had handed the Barrow gang over to the law in Drury.

'He said that you were on the trail of a man called Brady, and I happened to notice that the man next to me looked a mite shocked at the news he'd just heard. He left soon after. When I left myself, I noticed that a horse with a Double J brand, which had been standing at the hitching rail when I went into the saloon, was gone.'

'So Brady knows we're after him,' said Steve. 'Maybe he's expecting us to turn up here at the Crazy R. And it's likely the Double J hands are watching out for us.'

'Maybe so,' said Lee, 'though we ain't seen nobody over the last twenty miles or so. All the same, we'd better keep out of sight.'

'You're welcome to stay here,' offered Randle. 'You can sleep in the barn, and I'll ask the men not to mention to anybody that you're here.'

'We appreciate the offer,' said Lee, 'but if Brady and Jordan find out we're here, they're likely to cause you trouble.'

'I'm willing to risk that,' said Randle. 'I'd like to help you catch that murderer before he does any more killing. We'd like you to stay here till you've finished the job.'

'Thanks,' said Lee. 'If that's the way you feel, we accept the offer. What we have to do now is to start working on a plan to get our hands on Brady.'

'You four talk it over while Miriam and me get some supper on the go,' said Mary Randle. She and her daughter rose, and left to prepare the meal.

'The first thing we must do,' said Lee, 'is make sure that Brady is still at the Double J.'

'Maybe I can check up on that,' offered Tucker. 'I'm going into town on the buckboard with Miriam in the morning, for supplies. I'll check whether the man I saw in the saloon a few days ago has been seen in town again since then. And if he has been seen, maybe somebody will know if he's staying at the Double J.'

'That'll be a big help,' said Lee. 'Has Jordan got any friends in town?'

'I've got an idea,' Tucker replied, 'that a man called Miller, who works in the saloon in Purdy, is pretty thick with Jordan and his men. I've seen him talking with them in town, and a friend of mine saw him riding towards the Double J ranch house one day.'

The following morning, Miriam and Tucker left on the buckboard after breakfast, and Randle and his hands rode out on to the north range. Lee and Steve resigned themselves to waiting for the return of

Tucker and Miriam.

They were still waiting at three in the afternoon, and Mary Randle was getting worried. She spoke to Lee.

'Something's wrong,' she said. 'Miriam's never been anything like as late as this getting back from town.'

'We'll go out and look for them,' said Lee. He and Steve saddled their horses and rode along the trail towards Purdy.

They had ridden a little over three miles when they spotted the buckboard a short distance ahead, standing just off the trail. There was no sign of anyone on the driving-seat. Quickening their pace, they rode towards it.

As they came to a stop alongside it, they saw, lying among the supplies on the floor of the buckboard, the motionless body of Tucker, the foreman. Quickly, Lee dismounted and climbed on to the buckboard. He bent over the foreman.

There was blood on Tucker's vest, around the hole, high up on the chest, made by the bullet which was now lodged in the fore-man's body. Bending lower over the wounded man, Lee could see that he was still breathing. For a brief moment, his eyes opened, then closed again. Lee shook him gently, then patted his face, but the foreman's eyes remained closed.

'He's still alive,' said Lee to Steve, who was standing by the buckboard, 'but he needs a doctor bad. I don't reckon he can tell us just yet what happened to Miriam.'

He climbed down from the buckboard, and he and Steve closely examined the ground surrounding it.

'I reckon there were three riders here,' said Steve, 'and when they left they were heading north.'

'That's how I see it,' said Lee, then looked into the buckboard at Tucker. He was still unconscious. Lee noticed a folded sheet of paper sticking out of the foreman's vest pocket. He bent over to remove it, then unfolded it and read the message written on it in rough capital letters.

The message read:

WE HAVE THE GIRL. SHE STAYS ALIVE IF VICKERY AND NORTON COME UNARMED AND ALONE TO STEEPLE ROCK AT TEN TOMORROW MORNING. THEY MUST WAIT AT ROCKFALL ON SOUTH SIDE OF ROCK. IF THEY DON'T SHOW UP, OR TRY ANYTHING FOOLISH THE GIRL DIES. BRADY.

Lee handed the message to Steve, who read it, then looked into the worried face of his friend.

'You ride to Purdy, Steve,' said Lee, 'and ask the doctor to come out to the Crazy R ranch house to tend to Tucker. I'll take him there on the buckboard. We'll talk about tomorrow when you get back.'

Pete Randle and two of his hands rode in from the north range a short while before Lee arrived at the ranch house, driving the buckboard. Mary Randle, looking out through a window, saw it approaching. Her heart sank as she saw no sign of her daughter.

She called her husband, and they both ran out as the buckboard reached the house. They could see the wounded Tucker lying on the floor of the buckboard. Mary Randle ran over to Lee as he climbed down from the driving seat.

'Where's Miriam?' she asked.

Lee handed her the sheet of paper on which Brady's message was written. She and her husband read it together. Then Randle turned to look at Tucker.

'He's still alive,' said Lee. 'Steve's gone to Purdy for the doctor.'

'Bring him inside,' said Mary Randle, and Randle called two hands over to carry the wounded man to one of the bedrooms. When the two hands had left, Lee took off Tucker's vest and shirt, and Mary Randle cleaned the blood away, and had a look at the wound.

'There ain't nothing more I can do,' she said. 'We can only wait for Doc Sawyer.'

Then she saw that Tucker's eyes had

opened, and he was looking around. As he started to speak, the Randles and Lee leaned over him. His voice was barely audible.

'I'm sorry,' he said. 'There were three of them. They rode up from behind. One of them was Brady. One of the other two was Jordan's son, Roy. When I turned to speak to them, Brady shot me in the chest. Then they rode off, with Miriam and Brady riding double. They were heading north.'

His voice tailed off, and his head slumped forward.

'Hold on, Wes,' said Randle. 'Doc Sawyer's on his way.' But the foreman had once again relapsed into unconsciousness.

Leaving his wife to tend to Tucker, the rancher led Steve and Lee into the living-room.

'The most important thing is to get Miriam back,' said Lee. 'How many men does Jordan have on his payroll?'

'Around ten, I'd say,' Randle replied, 'and that's counting his foreman Nolan and his son Roy.'

'How old is the son?' asked Lee.

'Just over twenty, I'd say,' Randle replied. 'He's a wild one, hot-tempered, and spoilt by his father. Wears a couple of guns, with fancy holsters.

'Poor Miriam must be scared to death. Are you and your friend aiming to go to Steeple Rock tomorrow, like the message says?'

'Of course,' said Lee. 'We ain't got no option if there's to be any chance of getting Miriam back. But I don't trust Brady one little bit, and I'm beginning to get an idea of how we might get the better of him and Jordan. I'll talk it over with Steve as soon as he gets back. Meantime, can you tell me where Steeple Rock is?'

'Sure,' said Randle. 'It's south-west of here, about twelve miles away. It's a tall rock, tapering to a point at the top. It stands in the middle of a flat stretch of ground, so there's no chance of sneaking up on it under cover.'

He went on to mention a few landmarks to watch out for on the way.

When Doc Sawyer arrived with Steve

some time later, he hurried into the ranch house to take a look at the injured foreman. When he had finished his examination, he spoke to Randle and his wife, standing by the bedside.

'First thing to do is to get that bullet out,' he said. 'Judging by where it's gone in, I reckon that once I've managed to dig it out, there's a good chance that Wes'll be back to normal in a few weeks.'

Later, after he had extracted the bullet and bandaged the wound, the doctor spoke to the Randles.

'Mr Norton told me about Miriam,' he said, 'but he asked me not to say anything about it in town. I know you must be worried sick. What're you planning to do?'

'Lee and Steve are going to Steeple Rock tomorrow,' Randle replied, 'just like Brady told them to do in the message. Right now, they've got their heads together, trying to work out a plan for getting Miriam back, and saving their own lives as well. There's no doubt in their minds that Brady's figuring to kill them both.'

'I sure hope it all turns out right,' said Sawyer. 'I'll ride out tomorrow to see how Wes is doing.'

When the doctor had left, the Randles, both their faces lined with worry, joined Lee and Steve in the living-room. Mary Randle walked up to Lee.

'Can you get her back, Lee?' she asked.

'It's a pretty desperate situation,' Lee replied, 'and I can't tell you how sorry I am that you've been dragged into it. But Steve and me've been thinking up a plan that might upset Brady's plans.

'To make it work, Steve and me have got to ride out to Steeple Rock during the night, then come back here before dawn. And we've got to hope that one of the reception party waiting for us at the rock tomorrow is Jordan's son. We think he's likely to be there, because of his reputation. It's probably the sort of dirty operation he'd like to have a hand in.'

Steve and Lee discussed the plan with the

Randles for a while. Then, as darkness fell, they had a meal, and shortly after this, embarked on the ride to Steeple Rock. Watching out for the landmarks described earlier by Randle, they arrived at their destination before midnight.

The rock was about ninety feet high, with a roughly circular base, around a hundred feet in diameter. The steep sides rose to a sharp pinnacle at the top. They approached the rock with caution, then circled it, making sure that there were no men or horses anywhere near the base.

Circling the rock again, they located, on its north side, the rockfall mentioned in Brady's message. It was not a large fall, only about ten feet wide, and had obviously occurred some time ago. A patch of brush had grown over its foot.

Lee and Steve stayed there for a short while, then they returned to the Crazy R for a brief sleep before setting out for their confrontation with Brady and the others at Steeple Rock.

ELEVEN

Before leaving for Steeple Rock, Lee and Steve went to see Wes Tucker. The foreman was looking better, and they spoke with him for a few minutes about their plan to rescue Miriam. He voiced a fervent wish for the success of their mission.

Pete and Mary Randle went outside to see them off, and watched the two riders until they disappeared from view.

'Will we ever see them and Miriam again?' asked Mary Randle. Her voice was strained.

'I don't know,' her husband replied, 'but if anyone can save Miriam, I'm sure that those are the two to do it.'

A few minutes before two o'clock, Lee and Steve were approaching Steeple Rock from the northeast. No one was visible at its foot. They rode to within twenty yards of the rockfall, dismounted, walked up to it, and stood with their backs to it, about six feet apart.

A few minutes later, a man on foot appeared from behind the rock, to be followed by three others. Each of the four was holding a six-gun in his hand. Lee and Steve recognized two of them, from descriptions given, as Brady and Roy Jordan. They figured that the other two were Double J hands. It was Lee's first face to face encounter with the killer of his mother.

The four men stood side by side, facing Lee and Steve.

'Check them for weapons,' said Brady, to the two hands, 'and check them good.'

A thorough search of the two prisoners revealed no weapons, and the two hands rejoined Brady and Jordan. The four men holstered their guns.

Brady spoke to Lee. His voice was harsh.

'I'm tired of you following me, Vickery,' he said. 'You were a fool to think you could take me.'

Fighting to stay calm, Lee replied:

'I'm waiting to see the girl, Brady,' he said.

The four men laughed loudly.

'You're even more of a fool than I thought,' said Brady. 'Did you really think we'd bring the girl with us? She's back at the Double J. When I've got rid of you two, I'll have to think about what I'm going to do with her. She sure is a good-looker. Maybe I'll take her along with me.'

Miriam's absence was not entirely unexpected by Lee and Steve. They stood, motionless, facing their captors.

'As far as you two are concerned,' Brady went on, 'I can tell you exactly what's going to happen to you. I'm going to kill you both right here, then these men are going to help me to bury you some place away from here where you'll never be found. You'll just disappear. You got anything to say before you cash in?'

'Only,' said Lee, 'that I wonder if that's a posse coming up behind you.'

Startled, the men looked back over their

shoulders. As they did so, Lee and Steve half-turned, bent down, and plucked out of the patch of brush at the base of the rock-fall, one of the four six-guns which they had concealed there during the night, and whose locations they had carefully memorized.

Seeing no posse behind them, Brady and the others turned their heads back to look at Lee and Steve. Seeing, in shocked disbelief, the six-guns in their hands, they went for their own revolvers.

The ensuing gun battle was swift and decisive. With the advantage of surprise, Lee and Steve fired first at Brady and Jordan respectively, with time to select the points of impact of their bullets. Then, with no time to spare, they fired at the two hands, just before the latter had time to trigger their guns.

Brady and Jordan were both hit in the upper right arm; the hands were hit in the upper right shoulder. Each of the four had involuntarily dropped his gun before firing a shot.

Brady and Jordan were still standing. The other two had staggered back a few paces, and had then dropped to their knees. While Lee held a gun on them, Steve picked up their revolvers from the ground.

'We're going for a ride now,' said Lee, 'but before we start, you'd better take off your bandannas and try to stop the bleeding. It's going to be a while before anybody tends to those bullet wounds.'

Cursing, the four men did as Lee suggested, while Steve collected their horses from the far side of the rock. A little later, Steve and Lee helped the injured men into their saddles.

'We're heading for the Double J,' said Lee. 'You know the way. Let's get moving.'

'You don't think you're going to get away with this, do you, Vickery?' asked Brady. 'Jordan ain't going to take kindly to what you and your partner have just done.'

'I think we can make Jordan see reason,' said Lee. 'As for yourself, you're already on your way to the gallows in Amarillo. It won't be long before the rangers ride in to pick you up. And while we're on the way to the Double J, any of you causing any trouble is going to get another bullet in him.'

'It's a long way to Amarillo, Vickery,' said Brady, 'and maybe I'll get free on the way. If I do, there'll be no need for you to come after me, because *I'll* be coming after *you*. You can count on that.'

His voice was even, but there was a malevolent look in his eye that reminded Lee what an evil, ruthless killer this man was.

With the horses of the four prisoners roped together, and led by Lee, with Steve at the rear, they headed for the Jordan ranch. They halted as they came in view of the ranch buildings, in the early afternoon.

Steve stayed there with Brady and Roy Jordan, while Lee rode on with the two hands. As he drew closer to the ranch house, he saw several hands moving around. One of them ran to the ranch house door and disappeared inside. Moments later he reappeared with Cliff Jordan.

The rancher waited outside the house as Lee and the two wounded men rode up and stopped in front of him. Jordan looked past Lee towards the three distant, stationary riders. Several hands walked up and stood close by.

'Like you see, Jordan,' said Lee, 'things at Steeple Rock didn't go quite like you and Brady planned.'

Jordan glared at him.

'You've got a nerve, Vickery,' he said, 'riding in here like this. A word from me, and you're a dead man.'

'I don't think you're going to say that word,' said Lee, 'not so long as my friend back there is holding a gun on your son and Brady.'

Jordan looked at the three distant horsemen again, then spoke to one of the wounded hands.

'Is that Roy and Brady out there?' he asked.

The hand nodded. 'Yes,' he replied, 'and they're both plugged in the arm.'

193

'I know you've got the Randle girl here, Jordan,' said Lee, 'and the only way you're going to get your son back alive is by handing her over right now, in exchange for him. My friend out there knows what to do if he sees you making any move against me.'

'What about Brady?' asked Jordan.

'Brady stays with us,' Lee replied. 'He killed my mother, and he was ready to kill me and my partner today. We're handing him over to the law for trial.'

Jordan hesitated for a moment, then issued an order to two of the men standing by. They went into the ranch house, and came out a few minutes later with Miriam. She looked pale and distressed, but Lee could see no signs of violence on her. The men led her up to Jordan, to stand by his side.

'It's over, Miriam,' said Lee. 'You'll soon be home. Are you all right?'

'I'm all right,' she said. 'Apart from taking me away by force, they haven't harmed me.'

Lee turned to Jordan.

'What I'm going to do now,' he said, 'is ride back to my partner. Then I'll ride back with your son, and we'll stop when we're about two hundred yards from here. When I wave to you, Miss Randle will start walking towards me, and your son will start walking towards you. Any trickery, and I'll shoot your boy down with my rifle, and my partner will kill Brady.

'And I'd drop any idea you might have of rescuing Brady. If you try to take him from us before we reach town, we'll kill him. And after we've reached town, he's going to be very well guarded, and the rangers will soon be on their way to pick him up.'

'All right,' said Jordan. 'We'll play it your way.'

Lee rode out to Steve, then back with the rancher's son, to a point about two hundred yards from the ranch house. He dismounted, and told Roy Jordan to do the same. Then he waved to the rancher.

Miriam and the rancher's son started walking towards each other at the same time, and they crossed over midway between Lee and the rancher. When Miriam reached him, Lee could see the relief on her face.

'I sure was glad to see you turn up,' she said.

'Take Roy Jordan's horse,' said Lee, 'and we'll head for Purdy, then the Crazy R. Your folks have been mighty worried about you.'

He looked towards the ranch house. Jordan and his son had disappeared inside, and there was no indication that the rancher was sending men after them.

When they reached Purdy, they rode straight to the livery stable. Jarvis, the livery-man, was inside. He was surprised to see Lee and Steve again. Lee told him about the kidnapping of Miriam, and subsequent events.

He pointed to Brady.

'This is the outlaw Brady,' he said. 'He's the man who killed my mother, and who's responsible for the kidnapping of Miriam. Can we hold him in town somewhere, till the law gets here? I'm going to send a message to US Marshal Bantry in Amarillo.

He said he'd ask the Texas Rangers to send some men to pick up Brady, if ever we caught up with him.'

'We can hold him in the empty shed behind the stable,' said Jarvis, 'and I know I can find enough men willing to take a turn in standing guard. Now, about that message to the US marshal, you write it down, and I'll see that it's sent off as soon as possible.'

Lee wrote the message down on a sheet of paper supplied by Jarvis, and handed it to the liveryman.

'Tell everybody that Brady is a very dangerous man,' he said. 'Steve will stay here to organize the guard, while I take Miriam home. On the way out, I'll call and ask Doc Sawyer to take a look at Brady. And I'll tell him he'll likely be getting a call to the Double J pretty soon. I'll be back here in the morning.'

On the Crazy R, Mary and Pete Randle, who for some time had been watching anxiously for any sign of their daughter, ran out of the house as Lee and Miriam approached it, and dismounted. The rancher and his wife embraced their daughter, relieved that she appeared to be unharmed.

They all went inside, to be joined by Wes Tucker. Lee and Miriam gave their accounts of recent events.

'I don't expect any trouble from Jordan,' said Lee, 'but it might be a good idea for you and your hands to stay together near the ranch house for the next few days.'

Lee rode into Purdy the following morning, to help out with the guard that had been put on Brady. Steve told him that Doc Sawyer had been called out to the Double J the previous evening to attend to the gunshot wounds received by Roy Jordan and the two hands.

On the following day, word reached town that Jordan and his men had been seen driving a big herd of Double J cattle to the east, and that the Double J Ranch appeared to have been abandoned.

On the day after this news was received, a jail wagon rolled into Purdy, driven by

Ranger Price, with Ranger Nansen riding ahead. The wagon was basically a metal cage on four wheels, drawn by four horses. It already contained two prisoners, who had been picked up further north. They wore handcuffs and leg-irons.

Lee, standing with Steve outside the livery stable, saw the jail wagon approaching, and signalled it to stop. Ranger Nansen rode up to him.

'You Vickery?' he enquired.

Lee nodded. 'We've got Brady in a shed at the back,' he said. 'He was shot in the arm, but the doc says he's fit to travel.'

'Good,' said Nansen. 'We'll have a meal, then we'll head south for Amarillo. About the trial, our captain in Amarillo said you'd be wanted to give evidence. But he doesn't know when the trial's due to take place. When he does, he'll send you a message here.'

'All right,' said Lee, 'I'll stay around here till I get the message. I guess I don't have to warn you that Brady's a very dangerous prisoner. Killing don't mean nothing to him.'

'We know his reputation,' said Nansen, 'and I can tell you that the Ranger captain and US marshal in Amarillo were both mighty pleased to hear he'd been caught. Don't you worry none about us getting him to Amarillo. Price and me, we ain't lost a prisoner from a jail wagon yet.'

An hour later, Brady was shackled in the same way as the other two prisoners, and was locked in the jail wagon with them. Lee and Steve watched the wagon as it left town.

'Well, Steve,' said Lee, 'it looks like the job's finished at last. Thanks for your help. I couldn't have done it without you. What're you figuring to do now?'

'I've got an uncle who's ranching near Pueblo in Colorado,' Steve replied. 'I think I'll ride up there and pay him a visit. I'll leave in the morning. How about you?'

'I'll stay here till I get word from Amarillo about the trial,' said Lee. 'Maybe I can help out at the Crazy R while Tucker's laid up.'

'I can see why working at the Crazy R

would appeal to you,' grinned Steve. 'I can see you've really taken a shine to Miriam, and I can't think why, but it looks like she feels the same way about you.'

'I sure hope you're right,' said Lee, 'because I'm trying to work up enough courage to ask her to marry me.'

Steve left the following morning, and Lee rode out to the Crazy R, where Randle was grateful for his offer of help. He was working in the barn, when Miriam came in to see him.

'I'm glad the chase is over for you,' she said. 'When you were away, we were wondering if we'd ever see you again. Have you settled on what you're going to do when the trial's over?'

'That all depends on you,' said Lee.

'On me?' she said.

'If you say "yes" when I ask you to marry me,' said Lee, 'then you'll have a big say in what I'm going to do.'

'Was that a proposal I just heard?' she asked.

'It was,' said Lee. 'It's something I've been wanting to do ever since I first set eyes on you when you found me lying out on the range. I've only just whipped up the courage to do it.'

'The answer is "yes",' she said. 'I was getting round to thinking that maybe I'd have to do the asking myself.'

'You've made me a happy man, Miriam,' said Lee. 'D'you want me to have a word with your parents?'

'Leave it to me,' she said. 'I don't think they'll be all that surprised.'

Miriam knew that her parents were well aware of the strong mutual attraction between her and Lee. She also knew that they respected Lee, and was sure that they would be overjoyed at the proposed marriage.

They discussed the forthcoming wedding for a while, and decided that it would take place as soon as Lee had returned from his visit to Amarillo for the trial.

TWELVE

When the jail wagon left Purdy for Amarillo, good progress was made, and the day passed without incident. But on the morning of the following day, they had only covered a few miles when Price heard an ominous noise coming from one of the rear wheels. He stopped, and climbed down to take a look at it. Nansen joined him.

'I don't like the sound of it,' said Price. 'I'm sure it ain't just a shortage of axle grease. I reckon the wheel's damaged. And if you look close, you can see that the iron tyre on the wheel's starting to come loose.'

'I'm pretty sure,' said Nansen, 'that there's a small ranch just a few miles ahead. I reckon they'll be able to help us. Better take it slow till we get there.'

'All right,' said Price, and climbed back on

to the driving-seat. But they had only covered half a mile when suddenly, without any further warning, the rear wheel they had just been inspecting, collapsed.

The wagon lurched sideways at the rear, and veered right off the trail. The good rear wheel struck a rock which was deeply embedded in the ground, and rode up on to it. The wagon fell over on to its side, the tongue fractured, and the horses broke free.

As the wagon turned over, Price was thrown from the driving-seat to the ground, and the side of the wagon fell on to the lower half of his body, pinning him to the ground. Inside the wagon, the three prisoners were lying on the side of the cage.

Hearing the crash, Nansen rode back to the wagon, and knelt by the side of his partner. Price's face was distorted, and he was groaning with pain.

'Is it bad, Luke?' asked Nansen.

'It ain't good,' Price replied, his face beaded with perspiration. 'I reckon my legs are busted, and maybe that's not all. And the wagon's holding me down tight.'

Quickly, Nansen checked his six-gun, then went to the back of the wagon and unlocked the door of the cage. The three fettered prisoners, apparently unharmed, clambered out, and keeping a safe distance from them, Nansen directed them to the side of the cage where Price was lying.

'You men can see the situation here,' he said. 'I'm asking you to lift the wagon so's I can pull my partner out from under it. Any help you give me here will be mentioned to the judge at your trial.'

Suddenly, as the wagon shifted slightly, Price gave a scream of pain, then appeared to faint. As Nansen walked up to his partner and bent over him, Brady had a brief whispered conversation with the other two prisoners.

'We'll do it,' said Brady, as Nansen straightened up again, and looked at the prisoners. The ranger judged that the chain which was holding the hands of each prisoner together was long enough to allow them to attempt to lift the wagon.

He directed the prisoners to a point halfway along the side of the wagon, and knelt down, a few feet away from them, close to Price, ready to drag his partner free. His six-gun was in his hand.

He gave the word to the prisoners to start lifting. They were all strong men, and gradually they raised the wagon until it was clear of Price's body. Nansen told them to hold it in that position. Then, still grasping his six-gun, he took hold of his partner under the armpits.

But before he could start pulling, Brady muttered something to the two men standing by him, and all three released their hold on the wagon, which fell down again on the lower half of Price's body.

Instinctively, Nansen stood up and attempted to stop the wagon from falling back on his partner. By the time he realized the danger, it was too late. Moving with surprising speed for a man with shackled feet, Brady came up to Nansen from behind, and encircled his neck with the chain which was holding his hands together.

Pulling the chain tight, Brady held it so while Nansen vainly tried to free himself. Eventually, the ranger stopped struggling, and his body went limp. Giving a final sharp pull on the chain, Brady released his victim, and let him fall to the ground. He bent down, took Nansen's six-gun, and searched his pockets until he found the key for releasing the shackles. He also pocketed a roll of banknotes which the ranger was carrying.

Using the key, he released his own shackles. The other two prisoners shuffled up to him, and one of them held out his hand for the key.

'Not just yet,' said Brady, 'and keep your distance if you don't want a bullet in you.'

He pulled the clothes off Nansen, who was roughly his own height and build. Then he took off the distinctive prisoner's garb that he himself was wearing, and donned the dead ranger's clothing and gunbelt. He went for Nansen's horse, which was standing nearby. He mounted it and rode back to the two men standing by the wagon.

He took from his pocket the key for releasing the shackles, and threw it into a patch of brush twenty yards away. Then he rode off to the east, leaving behind him two men frantically searching in the brush for the key. By the time they found it he was well out of sight.

The news of Brady's escape reached the Crazy R the following day. A homesteader had come across the overturned wagon. Price and Nansen, the latter stripped of his clothing, were both dead. The three prisoners, together with Nansen's horse and two of the horses which had been drawing the wagon, were missing.

Inside the Crazy R ranch house, Lee and the Randles discussed the situation.

'I think,' said Lee, 'that after the threats made by Brady when we captured him, there's a strong chance that he'll come after me, and maybe Miriam as well. I reckon that Miriam and me should stay around the ranch house for the time being. And we'd better keep a close watch for Brady, day and night.'

'You're right,' said Randle. 'I'll get that organized right away.'

Four days after the prisoners escaped, Hiram Salter, a wandering prospector who had never lost confidence that there were still big finds to be made in the most unlikely places, was riding his mule eastward along a winding gully, about eight miles east of the Crazy R. A burro was trailing behind him.

Salter was a distant relative of Mary Randle, and he paid an occasional visit to the Crazy R. Miriam was a particular favourite of his. As he rounded a bend in the gully, he saw a rider coming towards him.

With a shock, he recognized the rider as Brady, whom he had recently seen in Purdy while picking up some supplies. He had been among the crowd watching Brady climb into the jail wagon.

He wondered how Brady could have escaped, and where he was heading. He suppressed all signs of recognition, as he stopped in front of the outlaw.

'Howdy, stranger,' he said.

'Howdy,' said Brady, taking a good look at Salter, and deciding that they hadn't met before. 'You heading east?'

'Only for a couple of days,' Salter replied, 'then I'm heading straight for Colorado.'

'I reckon you'll have a lot better chance of striking it lucky up there,' said Brady.

'Maybe so,' said Salter, and the two men parted.

Salter carried on for a few hundred yards, then stopped for a meal. After taking this, he rested for a couple of hours, then retraced his path along the gully until he emerged on to a stretch of flat ground. A careful scrutiny revealed no sign of Brady.

He headed for the Crazy R, arriving there late in the afternoon. Predictably, his news was received with considerable interest and concern, and the hands were all advised that

Brady was in the area. Salter asked if he could stay on at the ranch for a few days.

Lee already had the germ of an idea of how to deal with Brady, and after supper he sat down in the living-room with Salter, the Randles and Wes Tucker, to consider the matter. Salter's intimate knowledge of the surrounding area came in very useful.

As part of the plan eventually decided on, Randle went to Purdy the following morning. He rode up to the saloon, and went inside, to join six customers already there. Miller, the man he had previously suspected of passing information on to Jordan and Brady, was sweeping the floor. The rancher walked up to the bar, and stood in front of the barkeep. He called out to the customers.

'The drinks are on me, gentlemen,' he said. 'Miriam and Lee Vickery are figuring to get married, and there'll be a wedding as soon as we can get a preacher.'

The customers collected at the bar, and Randle called on Miller to join them. The barkeep handed out the drinks, poured one for himself, then spoke to the rancher.

'You having trouble getting a preacher, Mr Randle?' he asked.

'We've heard,' said Randle, 'that there's a wedding at Grindley's Bend, day after tomorrow. Lee's aiming to ride over on the morning of the same day, and fix it up with the preacher to marry him and Miriam as soon as he can.'

'I ain't never been to Grindley's Bend,' said the barkeep. 'What's it like?'

One of the customers cut in before Randle could reply.

'There's only five or six buildings,' he said. 'It's not far past Rattigan's Bluff.'

'That's right,' said Randle. 'The trail from here runs right close to the steep side of the bluff.'

'That outlaw Brady,' said the barkeep, 'd'you think he's likely to come looking for Mr Vickery?'

'Not a chance, according to Lee,' the rancher replied. 'Lee reckons that after what happened to Brady here, he'd be far too scared to come back.'

Randle left shortly after, and rode round to the back of the blacksmith shop. He asked the blacksmith, a friend of his, if he could keep watch on the street from a window in his living-quarters.

Forty minutes later he saw Miller leave the saloon, and walk over to the livery stable. A few minutes later he rode out on to the street. He passed in front of Randle, and rode out of town, heading east. The rancher went out on to the street, and watched Miller until he disappeared from view. Then he rode back to the Crazy R.

As Miller rode to the east, he stopped frequently to make sure he wasn't being followed. When he had covered just over eight miles, he veered to the right, and headed for a small ravine about half a mile off the trail.

As he entered the ravine, Brady stepped out from behind a boulder. He had been watching the approaching rider for some time, and was satisfied that he was not being followed.

'You got some news for me?' he asked Miller.

'I sure have,' Miller replied, and proceeded to tell the outlaw of Randle's visit to the saloon in Purdy, and of the ensuing conversation. Brady scowled as he heard of Lee's opinion that the outlaw would be too scared to return to the area.

'Maybe he'll change his mind,' he said, 'when I finally nail him. That trail to Grindley's Bend. D'you know it?'

'I know it well,' Miller replied, 'and when they mentioned Rattigan's Bluff, it struck me that there just couldn't be a better spot for an ambush. From the top of the cliff you can see the trail a long way back towards Purdy.'

'I've been trying to figure out,' said Brady, 'the best way of taking Vickery. It looks like you've given me the answer. I'll ride out there tomorrow. Is the bluff easy to climb on foot?'

'Yes,' Miller replied, 'the slope on the side opposite the cliff ain't all that steep.'

After giving Brady information on the best route to the bluff from the ravine, Miller said he had better return to Purdy before folks started wondering where he was.

'All right,' said Brady.

He pulled a wad of banknotes from his pocket, peeled off several, and handed them to Miller.

'That information you just gave me,' he said, 'is sure going to save me a lot of trouble.'

When Randle arrived back at the Crazy R after his visit to the saloon in Purdy, he told them how Miller had ridden out of town after hearing of Lee's proposed visit to Grindley's Bend.

'I think Brady's been in touch with Miller,' he said. 'Probably paid him a visit during the night. And I think Miller was riding out to see Brady at a hideout somewhere in this area.'

'Let's hope he takes the bait then,' said Lee, 'and decides on an ambush at Rattigan's Bluff. From what Mr Salter says, it looks like being an obvious choice for him. And it seems likely he'll ride out tomorrow, so's to be ready for me the day after.'

'Can I come with you, and bring a few men along?' asked Randle.

'No,' said Lee. 'It looks like Brady's on his own, and I aim to surprise him. There's a better chance of me doing that alone, and I don't want to run the risk of any of you being killed.

'If I manage to take him without a fight, I'd be glad of some help in holding him here till the rangers pick him up. And I might just ride with the jail wagon to Amarillo, to make absolutely sure he gets there this time.'

Miriam was silent. She was desperately worried about the dangers involved in Lee's plan to deal with Brady, but she knew that it was hopeless to try and change his mind.

Lee had a further talk with Salter about

Rattigan's Bluff and the surrounding area, then he turned in for a few hours' sleep. At three in the morning, he set off for the bluff. Miriam and her parents, all praying for his safe return, were there to see him leave.

Long before he reached it, Lee could see the bluff outlined against the night sky. Riding up to it, he circled the bluff and found no evidence of anyone else being there.

When daylight came, he found a place to tether and conceal his horse on the side of the bluff which was not visible to anyone coming along the trail from Purdy. He then found a crevice, at the foot of the cliff, in which he could stand, concealed, while watching out for the arrival of Brady.

Two hours after the arrival of Lee at Rattigan's Bluff, Brady left the ravine where he was hiding out, and headed for the same destination. He aimed to arrive there with plenty of time to look around and decide on the best place to lie in ambush for Lee.

As he approached the bluff, observed by Lee in his hiding-place, Brady could see that a position on top of the cliff was a perfect location for a rifleman wishing to shoot down a rider approaching along the trail from Purdy.

When he reached the bluff, he dismounted, about sixteen yards from Lee, and stood looking up the face of the cliff. Then he turned, so that his back was to Lee, with the intention of walking along the cliff face.

Lee stepped out of the crevice, holding his Peacemaker, ready to call on Brady to raise his hands. Then, at exactly the wrong moment, Lee's horse neighed, the sound carrying clearly to Lee and the outlaw.

Brady twisted round, drawing his six-gun. Startled at the sight of Lee in front of him, he fired, just as the bullet from Lee's Peacemaker ploughed into his heart. He fell to the ground.

Lee was more fortunate. He had a flesh wound in the side. He was sure there was no bullet inside him, but the wound was bleeding freely. He decided to ride to the Crazy R, where Miriam would be waiting so anxiously for his return. He figured he could make it. When he got there, he would ask Randle to have Brady's body picked up. He made a pad to hold against the wound, went for his horse, and headed for the ranch.

Miriam was the first to see him. She had been watching through a window for the past two hours. She stiffened as a distant rider came into view. The horse was moving slowly, not in a straight line, and the rider seemed to be slumped forward in the saddle.

Miriam's parents, seated in the same room, looked up as their daughter suddenly turned from the window, rushed out of the room, then out of the house. Seeing a saddled horse near the bunkhouse, she ran up to it, leapt into the saddle, and headed at full speed for the distant rider.

Randle and his wife hurried out of the house after Miriam. Looking beyond her they could see the distant horseman. The horse was now stationary, and the rider appeared to have collapsed over the neck of his mount.

They ran to the buckboard, which had just returned from town, and followed Miriam. When they reached her, she was standing by the horse, holding Lee to prevent him falling from the saddle. They helped her to ease him down to the ground. His eyes opened as the Randles bent over him.

'Brady's finished,' he said, weakly. 'I left him at the bluff. I got hit in the side, but I don't think it's serious. It's been bleeding bad, and I reckon I've lost a lot of blood, is all.'

They lifted him on to the buckboard, and took him to the ranch house. Randle sent a hand to Purdy for Doc Sawyer, and another two to Rattigan's Bluff to collect Brady's body and his horse, and take them to Purdy.

When the doctor arrived, he confirmed that Lee's wound was not serious, and should heal up without complications. When

Sawyer had gone, Miriam sat with Lee for a while.

'Well, Miriam,' he said, 'now we can talk about our future without worrying about Brady. I reckon we should marry just as soon as the doc allows me out of this bed. As to what we do after that, what d'you think of the idea of us running the Box V Ranch near Bledsoe that belonged to my father?

'It ain't all that far from here, so you could see your folks regular. It'll need licking into shape again, but that won't take long. In no time at all, we'll be raising cattle there, and maybe a youngster or two as well.'

'I'm all in favour of the idea,' said Miriam, 'especially the last part. Just you hurry up and get better as quick as you can.'

Three weeks later they were married, and three days after that, they headed north for the Box V.

The publishers hope that this book has given you enjoyable reading. Large Print Books are especially designed to be as easy to see and hold as possible. If you wish a complete list of our books please ask at your local library or write directly to:

Dales Large Print Books
Magna House, Long Preston,
Skipton, North Yorkshire.
BD23 4ND

This Large Print Book, for people
who cannot read normal print,
is published under the auspices of
THE ULVERSCROFT FOUNDATION

... we hope you have enjoyed this book.
Please think for a moment about those
who have worse eyesight than you ...
and are unable to even read or enjoy
Large Print without great difficulty.

You can help them by sending a
donation, large or small, to:

**The Ulverscroft Foundation,
1, The Green, Bradgate Road,
Anstey, Leicestershire, LE7 7FU,
England.**
or request a copy of our brochure for
more details.

The Foundation will use all donations
to assist those people who are visually
impaired and need special attention
with medical research, diagnosis
and treatment.

Thank you very much for your help.